WHEN IT'S LOVE

A Silver Pines Christmas

GWEN HAYES

This is a work of fiction. Similarities to real people, places, or events are entirely coincidental.

WHEN IT'S LOVE

Copyright © 2016 Gwen Hayes.
Written by Gwen Hayes.

Excerpt from ALL I NEED

Copyright © 2016 Gwen Hayes.
Written by Gwen Hayes.
ISBN: 1539985903
ISBN-13: 978-1539985907

ALSO BY GWEN HAYES

SILVER PINES SERIES

Don't Stop Believing
Need You Tonight
When It's Love
All I Need (coming 2017)

CAMP FIREFLY FALLS

Winning Back His Wife
His Counterfeit Campfire Bride
His Runaway Campfire Princess (Coming 2017)

Chapter One

AGAINST ALL ODDS, it is possible to feel lonely in a room full of people you love.

Lisa Rhodes kept herself busy-looking by adjusting the pine garland across the mantle of her childhood home. "Busy-looking" was a trick. A trick she'd honed from childhood. It was her way of hiding in plain sight. If you're busy, or at least look busy, most people leave you alone. At least for a while.

Bing Crosby crooned in the background while she placed sprigs of holly berries, pine cones, and baby's breath evenly down the twelve-foot garland. It had to be perfect. Not because anyone cared—her large, boisterous family wasn't concerned with the concept of perfection—no, it needed to be perfect because she'd spent so damn long arranging it now that she'd feel stupid if it didn't look right. Around her, the family was busy with other decorations in the great room and ...beer. Beer was a definite activity, as per usual. Her mother was in the kitchen baking more cookies than a Keebler Elf did in his entire lifetime. Judging by the yelling directed at the television, her siblings and cousins were upset with the scores of some game and what kind of intervention the refs needed due to some play or another.

Honestly, she had no idea. Sportsing all sounded the same to her. But it wouldn't be long before all the joking and conversation rounded the room to her. *Who are you dating? Why aren't you dating?* She'd smile awkwardly and someone would call her shy and then she'd blush and that would start another set of discussion points about her appearance. They loved her and the teasing was always good natured. But it was still teasing. She felt silly for feeling like she didn't fit in, but even now, at twenty-five years old, she felt out of place in the bustle of her huge family.

Lisa was child number four of four—two sets of twins for her parents—and one of innumerable cousins—including honorary ones—because apparently, they couldn't have a family large enough. She loved them, all of them, she just preferred them one at a time. She wasn't shy, not really. She simply felt overwhelmed in groups. Especially the last few years.

Being the focus of attention had always been uncomfortable for her, but her siblings thrived on it—each of them good at sports and performing. Lisa was good at...being Lisa. She liked her quiet apartment in town. Her quiet job for her grandparents. Her quiet life crafted with just the right balance of solitude and family.

But today was a good day. It wasn't Christmas for another week, but today was even better than Christmas. Ben was coming home.

She checked the time. Not long now.

Ben Rhodes, her twin, was the exception to the "family makes me feel weird" rule. He'd just finished his second tour in Afghanistan and this would be his first Christmas home in a few years. Consequently, the celebration of Christmas was slated to be more like a weeklong festival this year. Mom was determined to make up for his lost Christmases.

While having a big family already meant lots of traditions, it seemed like this year was going to go off the rails into Christmas mania. Her mother had actually been taking notes on a legal pad while watching *The Santa Clause*. Notes. Probably things like "source a reindeer" or "pay the town's children to dress up like elves."

Ben would love it. All of it. Lisa supposed a reindeer wouldn't be so bad. And she liked kids. Just not a lot of them in a small space. But she wasn't crazy about the figgy pudding. Mom sent an email last week putting her in charge of it. For fifty people. That was a lot of figgy. That was a lot of people.

But Lisa was *so* looking forward to having Ben home.

It had been hard without him the last few years. Probably good for her in a lot of ways. But he was her twin. Her other half. They could communicate without words and nobody made her laugh like he did. Skype was a poor substitute.

The game switched to a commercial break, so Lisa slipped into the kitchen and took a deep breath. So far so good for avoiding the awkward dating conversations.

"Just in time," her mom said. "The cookies are ready to decorate."

Lisa looked at the shapeless cookies lining the counter. She held one up to the light, wondering why it had a hole in the middle of what could have maybe been a snowman. "Mom, they let you cut people open for a living. Why can't you cut a cookie? These don't...what are they supposed to look like?"

"I can't figure out what I'm doing wrong either. Every year, I roll the dough, I cut the dough, but by the time I get them into or out of the oven, they look more like Patrick Star than trees and Santas."

Lisa picked another one up. "This one is more Spongebob than Patrick."

"Ha-ha."

They'd worked side-by-side for half an hour when her mom got the text that they were almost home. "Did you put the guest towels out?"

"Yes, Mom." She'd already asked twice today.

"Not the *nice* guest towels...the fancy ones."

Lisa got prickles on the back of her neck. "Why would we put the fancy guest towels out for Ben? I mean, I know we missed him, but he's still *Ben*." Not *fancy* guest towel material.

"He's bringing his sergeant home with him. Or ex-sergeant. I'm not sure how that works. He's the one who saved your brother's life, but he's getting out of the army now. Sergeant Carter."

Fabulous. One more person. And a stranger to make it interesting. *Breathe. Just breathe.*

Lisa took the bowls to the sink so she could talk without having to look directly at her mother. It might be easier to approach her about the sleeping arrangements without eye contact. "Mom, I've been thinking. Maybe I should stay in town this week after all. It sounds like you're going to have a full house here. There's no reason why I can't stay in my own apartment." *Where there are no strangers.* "I'll commute here every day."

She chanced a glance behind her. Her mom had that look—the one that said "What are we going to do with you, Lisa?"

"What? I just think—"

"Your father and I are really looking forward to having all of you home. Under one roof. For the week. Like old times."

Lisa had taken a week's vacation and she and her siblings had all "moved" home for the holiday. She missed her quiet apartment already and she'd only been home for a few hours. "I'll come back first thing every morn—"

"Please, Lisa. We all need this. As a family. There is plenty of room here, and I don't want to worry about you driving home late at night."

"Late at night?" Why would she be up late at night?

Her mother took the rinsed bowls and put them into the dishwasher. "We have things scheduled every evening this week."

"Scheduled?"

Mom nodded towards the fridge while she added soap to the dispenser. "It's on the itinerary. I was going to pass copies of it out later, but there's one on the fridge if you want a sneak peek."

"You have an itinerary?" Lisa took the paper off the fridge. "You have a *typed* itinerary. Mom this is in outline format. With Roman numerals."

"It needed to be organized. We are having an old-fashioned family Christmas and you are all going to look back on this time and be grateful we were together."

Alrighty then. Her mother had become Clark Griswold.

"Mom..."

Her mother's phone buzzed and she picked it up after shooting Lisa a quelling glance. "They're here."

Chapter Two

SERGEANT JOE CARTER sat in the backseat of the Escalade and watched the freeway turn into a highway turn into one single main street that ran through the entirety of Silver Pines, Washington. The gray December clouds made it impossible to tell the time of day, but he knew it shouldn't have been dark enough for all the streetlights to be on yet. It wasn't raining, exactly, more like the sky was spitting at the car as they crawled down the street. Some hail, some rain, some mist, maybe even a little snow, but not the kind that stuck.

Mr. Rhodes—Mark he'd said to call him—was driving them home from the airport. Well, he was driving his son home. Joe didn't have a home or a clue as to whether or not he even wanted one or how to go about finding one if he did. He hadn't stayed anywhere that wasn't Army issued in a long-ass time. He was tagging along for the ride.

Roadie...no Ben—he was supposed to call him Ben now—had family connections to Stone Rhodes, a custom garage in Silver Pines that specialized in restoring muscle cars and had a reputation for quality that was unmatched anywhere else in the country. Joe had put in an order for his dream car, a '67 Chevy Camaro. Roadie had gotten him a great deal with the understanding that Joe would come home with him and spend the holidays with his family. It was a pity-invite, but Roadie was a good guy and Joe wanted that car.

"On your right is my high school, Sarge. Silver Pines only has two schools—K-6 and 7-12."

Joe barely remembered high school, but there were probably more kids in his Chicago graduating class than in both Silver Pines schools combined. "Not your sarge anymore." Joe was officially out now. Retired. Unshackled. Unmoored.

Adrift.

"I don't think I can call you Joe," Roadie answered. "Too used to Sarge."

"Yeah, *Ben* is going to be a stretch for me, too."

They laughed and Ben's dad filled Joe in on town trivia as they turned onto Bear Mountain Road. Joe had heard a lot of the stories before. In the sandbox, home was a popular topic for many of the enlisted men. Ben had never told him about Ironwing, though.

"I think I've heard the name Ironwing. Hair band from the 80s, right?" Joe asked. "I think I remember one song."

Mark laughed. "I guess they were a one-hit-wonder group. They never recorded anything after the one album. But Ironwing is the only thing Silver Pines is famous for. Jason Stone, the guy who's working on your dream wheels, is the son of the bass player. He's also the sheriff."

Jason Stone must be the *Stone* in Stone Rhodes. And a busy man. Joe figured Mr. Rhodes must not know the reputation for the garage or he'd have counted that as something else Silver Pines is famous for.

"Jason's like family," Roadie added. "It's a long story, but he and his two sisters are honorary cousins. He'll do a great job on your car. You'll meet him today."

They pulled into the circular drive of a large log cabin. Huge windows and glass doors made up the front, and a wide porch wrapped around the house like a protective embrace. Joe whistled out a breath. He knew Rhodes had come from a very comfortable upbringing—his dad was a lawyer, his mom a doctor, and his grandparents owned the town car lot as well as the custom garage. They weren't millionaires or anything, Joe didn't think, but the house was significant and picture perfect. If L.L. Bean wanted to film a commercial, the Rhodes homestead would be the perfect place for it. Joe hadn't realized that there were people who lived life like the magazines and catalogs showed. Not really.

The outdoor white Christmas lights twinkled against all the gray. Huge red ribbon bows festooned the porch rails, but you couldn't miss the bigger yellow bow on the door. Ben Rhodes had been missed. He'd been thought of every day.

The three of them got out of the car as the front door opened and people poured out. Roadie's family gathered around him, their voices raising to be heard above the ones just joining. People were still spilling out the front door.

Joe hung back, allowing the crowd better access to their returning soldier. He inhaled deeply. The air smelled clean. Fresh. He didn't want to exhale and poison it with the breath from his lungs. He suddenly wished very much to go back to the place where everything was khaki and camouflage. Where a guy like him felt safe.

It was then he noticed he wasn't the only one hanging back. One woman stood on the empty porch and leaned against the rail. Waiting.

She was dressed in brown and gray, practically a chameleon against the wood and the weather. He suspected that was on purpose. A camouflage like he was used to. Her clothes, the shape of them, the way they hid her body, said she was middle aged, but having spent too many years where danger came from people trying to look safe, he didn't stop his inspection there. Assumptions about people based on what they wanted you to see first could get you killed.

Her face was unlined and fresh, at odds with her clothing. Her hair was pulled back in a ponytail or braid, but soft wisps of blonde curls escaped and softened the look. She might even be pretty. But it was obvious she didn't want people to work that out on their own. She waited patiently as the mob scene got louder. When a smile bloomed across her face, Joe followed her gaze to Roadie.

They shared the same smile. *She must be Roadie's twin*. Joe had heard about her. Lisa was her name, if he recalled correctly. Roadie always claimed she was the better half of the duo. He'd said she was the quiet one, and Joe could tell by her appearance that was not an exaggeration. What else had he said? That they had a connection. That ever since they were kids, they always knew exactly what the other needed.

Rhodes broke away from the crowd and made short work of the distance between the car and the porch. Her smile transformed her face, and she took the steps quickly and launched herself into her brother's arms. That smile. God.

Rhodes twirled her around, and when he stopped, she cupped his face in her hands and wept while she laughed.

Joe thought he should look away. The moment felt too personal. But he was transfixed. Nobody had ever wept for him. Laughed for him. Did Roadie know how lucky he was?

The pack moved towards Joe, and Mark began a flurry of introductions. Joe lost sight of the twins and put on his game face. Polite he could do. He'd have to be careful with his language. He didn't expect that civilians would care for the way most soldiers spoke their minds. Bluntly would be an understatement. But since he wasn't a talkative man, he figured he'd be all right. And he needed to learn to fit in. This was life now.

The family surrounding him was more than nice, and it was easy to play along, but what he really wanted to do was be alone.

Except that wasn't true either. He had no idea how to be alone. He'd been part of a team for so long, yet he'd always felt apart. It was easier to deal with the feeling when he had a job, responsibilities. He'd cared about his men, his team. He was shocked to find he was unprepared for not having anyone to care about, even if the feelings weren't returned.

But he was used to feeling lonely even when surrounded by people.

Chapter Three

LISA COULDN'T SLEEP.

She missed her own bed. Her adult bed. Sleeping in her childhood room was just weird. She'd crashed at her parents' home before, but this time it was different. Like premeditated regression. Her room wasn't exactly a shrine, but it certainly hadn't been changed very much either.

So, she did what any grown up would do, she headed to the kitchen to eat cold pizza and raid her dad's whiskey at two in the morning.

She left the lights dim, enjoying the glow from the strings of multicolored lights she and her sister Amy had wrapped around pine boughs and then draped on top of the cupboards. She ate her pizza and then turned her attention to her beverage, remembering the first time she and Ben had stolen booze from the liquor cabinet and how not great that turned out. They had tried to replace the vodka in the bottle with water, but got busted when her parents decided to put the vodka in the freezer before a summer party and their "booze" froze.

Not the first or last time she and Ben had been in double trouble.

Lost in her thoughts, Lisa felt his presence before she saw him—the infamous Sergeant Carter. She stiffened and turned toward the door. There he stood, arms braced across the doorway, his masculine shape redefining all her previously held impressions of her mother's kitchen.

Wow.

He was wearing a simple tank top and his army-issued sweatpants hung loosely on his hips. The way he held his arms left no need to imagine the curves and planes of his strong muscles and shoulders. As she had totally done all through dinner. Her imagination was no match for reality.

He tilted his head, asking permission to enter, so she sent him a small smile. Her mouth felt too dry to form a verbal response.

Just wow.

When her mom had said Ben was bringing home his retiring sergeant, Lisa had assumed someone much older. Someone grizzled and gray. But this guy was probably in his mid-thirties and the most prime-of-his-life specimen she'd ever been privileged to see in person. Well over six feet with dark eyes that promised danger. His cheekbones were chiseled, able to cut into a girl's heart for sure, and just a scrape of stubble rasped across them. He'd probably shave that off in the morning. Or maybe he wouldn't.

She wondered how long it would take for him to ease up on his military rules of appearance. She guessed a long time.

"Can't sleep, Joe?" she asked, sliding the pizza box over a place setting on the counter for him.

He joined her, taking the second stool at the breakfast bar next to her. "It's too quiet."

Lisa grabbed a Santa cup off the mug tree and poured some whiskey into it for him. He huffed a small grateful laugh and thanked her. His large hands wrapped around the mug and made her quiver a little.

Get a grip, Lisa.

They sat in silence for a few moments while he ate a slice and she sipped her whiskey. She didn't know what to say. She wasn't good at ice-breaking. If they had something in common, it would be easier. But all they had was Ben.

He cleared his throat. "You're wearing red."

Well, that was an interesting ice breaker, but probably no less weird than what she'd have come up with on her own. She looked down at her long underwear shirt and plaid jammie bottoms. "Yes. I'm wearing red." Time for another sip.

She met his eyes over the rim of her cup, and they were taking her in from head to toe. It was disconcerting. Most guys didn't notice her these days.

"I'm just surprised. Red is a standout color."

She jerked back involuntarily. Oh. *Oh*. "Red is a Christmas color." Was she not supposed to stand out?

"Easy, mistletoe." He put a hand on her arm to stop her from retreating. "I didn't mean it in a bad way. From what I saw at dinner, from the pictures of you around the house, you don't wear bright colors. You like to blend." He paused. Like maybe he hoped that was enough of an explanation. Then sighed. "I'm not good at this, am I?" She looked down at his hand, and he removed it quickly. "I was trying to say that red looks nice on you and you should wear it more often. I don't usually have such a problem talking to women, but I've been blowing it with you all night. I'm sorry."

First, her mind got stuck on the part where he noticed what she wore at all. Much less pictures of her. And then it caught up and latched onto the last thing he said. "What do you mean you've been blowing it with me all night?"

His eyes widened in the only amount of panic she'd probably ever see on his face. Sometimes, boys were really ridiculous. She was hardly scary. "Look, I can tell you don't like me."

"I hardly know you. What makes you think I don't like you?"

He shrugged and started tracing the top of his mug with his finger. The action should not have made her nipples tighten under her long johns. She pulled her eyes away from the mug.

"You just don't seem to. At dinner...after dinner when we were all in the living room...I thought you were angry or something. Or that I rubbed you the wrong way, no matter what I said."

She sank all the way back onto the stool. Reaching

for the whiskey, she said, "That's not true. I'm just quiet. Usually people just call me shy. I've never been accused of being a snob before."

"I didn't say you were a snob."

She wasn't shy, either. She just didn't like being noticed. She'd never really thought that maybe by trying so hard to be unnoticed, she might be drawing even more attention to herself.

But none of that was Joe's fault.

She was about to say something polite when she remembered he'd given her a nickname. "Did you really just call me *mistletoe*?"

"Seemed like a good idea at the time." He tipped his mug for a refill. "So, my guess is that we are the two worst communicators currently in residence."

She poured, grateful for something to do. "And here we are with no backup." This awkward encounter was not getting any less awkward. She took a sip of the whiskey. "I'm much better with people one on one than I am in a crowd. I was just being quiet tonight. It wasn't personal. Let's start over." She pointed to his cup. "Hi, my name is Lisa. Can I buy you a drink in this bar in the middle of nowhere?"

Lame. Geez.

He scrunched his brows together and then shook his head. Confused, because duh, she was so weird. Then he grinned. "Hi Lisa. I'm Joe. Where I come from, men buy the pretty ladies a drink. Come here often?"

She giggled. In spite of herself. In spite of the fact that there were no nearby rocks to crawl under.

"New in town. You?"

"Here on business. I'm a…" Joe looked around the kitchen, his eyes resting on the stove. "I'm a …pot holder salesman. From Kansas."

"Pot holders? That's fascinating." She took another sip. "I bet you are very influential in your company."

He nodded, a smile breaking out a dimple she hadn't realized he had. "I'm kind of a big deal."

Joe held up his hand like he was getting the bartender's attention and indicated two more drinks.

"Oh, I shouldn't," she said, while pushing her cup towards him for more.

"Tell me what you do," he said as he poured their drinks. "Before I do something stupid and ask you what a pretty girl like you is doing in a place like this."

He already knew she was a bookkeeper for her grandparents, as that had come up at dinner. "I'm a singer. Karaoke champion in four counties."

He laughed, a nice rumble that she felt strumming in her own belly and then lower. "Look at us. We haven't offended each other for several minutes."

He smelled really good. When he cocked his head in question, she realized she'd said that out loud.

Well, since it was a day that ended it "Y" it was hardly surprising that she embarrassed herself. "Sorry. I…don't get out much." She'd been drinking, yes, but she wasn't drunk.

He laughed again. "You smell good, too." He was

teasing, but it was nice. "Your hair...I like it down."

She patted her somewhat crazy curls and bit her lip. Which brought his attention to her mouth until he brought his gaze back up to her eyes.

The air felt charged, a moment dragging impossibly long between them. Like static buzzing and zapping. She couldn't look away from his eyes even though she knew she'd been staring into them too long. It was like falling. Or maybe flying.

"I should go," he said, but he didn't look away. God, he was absolutely the most handsome man she had ever seen in person.

"If we were really in a bar, would you try to get me to leave with you?" That was really a stupid question. One that she didn't want to know the answer to.

Joe swallowed hard. "We're not in a bar, though. You're my buddy's sister, and I'm in your parents' kitchen."

"You didn't answer my question."

"Lisa, you're a nice girl."

Well, *that* answered the question, didn't it? Nice girl was shorthand for plain. Simple. Not the girls you pick up in a bar.

She shouldn't have felt let down. She'd spent the last two-and-a-half years cultivating plain and simple. She tried very hard not to look like a girl who could be picked up in a bar. Not to *be* a girl who got picked up in a bar. She'd embarrassed herself and her family enough this decade.

But it stung just the same.

She sucked at handling rejection. Even before the *incident*. After... well she spent a lot of time making sure not to put herself in rejection's path.

She got up and busied herself with putting the pizza box away and rinsing her cup. He hadn't left the kitchen, so she had to fake being fine. She wasn't sure she was pulling it off.

"Lisa." He was directly behind her. He'd moved like a ninja or something.

She closed her eyes. "Hmm?"

With one big hand on her hip, he turned her around until they were face to face, barely an inch between them. The heat of his palm scorched beneath the pajama pants. "You're a very pretty girl."

She snorted and tried to turn, but he cupped her chin and brought her back to his dark, hot gaze. "If we were in a bar, I would have worked every angle until I got you back to my hotel room."

Her breath hitched. "I probably wouldn't have been interested," she lied.

This time he snorted. "Oh, you're interested."

"You think highly of yourself," she balked. *Also, you're right.*

"Some things are inevitable. But I'm going to try really hard to put this one off."

"Right. Inevitable. So inevitable that you can walk away. I get it. I'm not your type. You don't have to give me excuses—"

He stopped her with his mouth. A hot, wet zing that went straight from her lips to the center of her body and then lower. He still held her face in one hand, and his other squeezed her hip. Holding her still. He liked being in charge.

She really liked him being in charge.

Joe slanted his lips over hers and coaxed her mouth open. He tasted like the whiskey they'd shared, and she drank him in, getting more intoxicated with each pass of his tongue. He paused, pulling back to look into her eyes. Then he closed his own, exhaling a sigh as he pressed his forehead to hers.

"I'm sorry."

"No, you're not." *Please don't be sorry.*

"No, I'm not." He stepped back. "But I'm just passing through. I'm too old for you. I'm not boyfriend material, and you deserve better. Also, your brother will kill me."

Lisa couldn't help but laugh. "I'm not going to tell him. Are you?" He still looked uncomfortable. "Look," she said. "We got carried away. Lost in a moment. Blame it on the mistletoe."

"We're not standing under mistletoe."

"Right. Well, then it's the Christmas lights. And the whiskey. And the time of year. You're home safe from war. Whatever."

He didn't look convinced, but he nodded. She lifted to her tiptoes and kissed his cheek before she practically ran out of the kitchen.

Because while she knew it could be any or all of those reasons, she was afraid it was the one she didn't say. That despite everything she'd done, no matter how hard she'd tried to hide her body, her looks, Alan was right that night two-and-a-half years ago. That his words were true then and true now.

You're a slut.

Chapter Four

DURING A HUGE breakfast of bacon, eggs, pancakes, hash browns, and freshly-squeezed orange juice, Mrs. Rhodes handed out to-do lists to her children and asked Joe to go with Ben and Lisa. After being treated to a meal that almost made him forget he'd ever had to eat an MRE, he didn't feel like he could tell Mrs. Rhodes no to anything ever again, but he was worried about any awkwardness for Lisa.

Damn. He still didn't know what came over him last night. He just couldn't watch her shrinking the way she had been. It was more than just her being introverted, hell, he was just as bad about being social as she was. No, it was something different. She had been withdrawing into herself like she thought there was something wrong with her, and no way Joe could let her think that.

She could dress as plain and simple as she

wanted, but it didn't change the fact that she was beautiful. It wasn't the kind of beauty that smacked you with glamour. It was quiet, luminous. And if other guys couldn't see past her outfits, that was on them, not her. She had a quality he'd never come across before—and her brother was right about her. She was special. She deserved a smart guy who would get to know her before he made judgments about what kind of woman she was.

He still wasn't sure why she protected herself with boring, shapeless clothes, but underneath, she was warm and sexy and she deserved to know that. The way she'd kissed him back, melting in his mouth and twining around his body, he had no doubts she was made to be pleasured.

But she also needed the guy that figured that out to not be someone like him.

She was no quieter in the car than she had been the previous night at dinner, but Joe couldn't deny that part of him hoped she would have felt more comfortable with him. Like she had been when they were talking alone. Two strangers in a bar. But he'd ruined that when he kissed her, and it was his own damn fault. He was lucky she hadn't told her brother what a jackass he'd been. By all rights, he should have been kicked out and banished to the streets of Silver Pines by the Rhodes family for disrespecting their daughter like that.

And he began to wonder why she hadn't told her twin what had happened. Roadie had told him more than once how his sister was his best friend. If she kept things like last night from Roadie, how was the guy supposed to protect his sister? Joe started getting mad at her for not telling. She shouldn't keep things like that from her family. What if he were a different kind of man? One who took her quiet as permission? One who cared more about getting laid than her feelings or his friendship with her brother? One who used her or even hurt her?

He shook his head when he realized that he wanted to kick his own ass on her behalf.

The whole situation was messed up.

They parked on a street that still had angled parking. Rhodes handed the keys to Lisa after popping the back open. "Would you two mind taking the boxes to the library for Mom on your own?" he asked. "I have some shopping left to do."

Lisa clapped and smiled. "Yay! That means he's shopping for me." She got out of the car and went to the trunk where Rhodes handed her a box. "Don't do all your shopping at the hardware store this year, 'k?"

"Hey, everyone should have their own set of tools. Even bratty sisters."

"I have two brothers. What do I need with tools? Something breaks, I call you guys."

Rhodes tugged her braid as Joe grabbed the other box. He guessed she was probably too independent to call her brothers for every little thing and that she'd probably made use of the tools. But even Joe knew that was a boneheaded gift.

"Come on, Joe. The library is this way." She started walking, so he nodded a quick goodbye to Roadie. Rhodes. *Ben.*

The street reminded him of Bedford Falls from *It's a Wonderful Life*. He'd seen the movie every year since enlisting thanks to the sentimental saps he worked with. After about the fifth time seeing it, it became a tradition he looked forward to. Like a hot dog on the 4th of July or turkey—or what passed for turkey in the mess hall—on Thanksgiving.

Old fashioned lamps decorated with wreaths lined the sidewalks in front of the Victorian shop fronts. A grassy median lined with oak trees gave the appearance of a different, slower time. But it was the shop windows that drew his attention. Some of them projected out with white panes—but all of them showcased a Christmas scene. Glitter, lights, baubles, toys...and since there were no cars on this part of the street, he really could have stepped into a different era.

When he caught up to Lisa after pulling himself away from a Santa's Workshop scene, he asked, "Hey why are we bringing books to the library, anyway? Doesn't it usually work the other way?"

"These are for the Christmas party. Santa gives each child a book for a gift. My parents purchase them every year for donation. The librarian will curate them for the different age groups."

"Your family is pretty great," he said, liking that she hadn't clammed up on him. Maybe they could be friends. He'd had a couple female friends in the Army, but never a civilian one. The women he met on leave were nice, but he'd never classify them as friends.

"We've been fortunate. My parents always taught

us to pay it forward. Give back. But yeah, they are pretty great."

She smiled at him, and he almost dropped his box. It was like the one he'd seen her give her brother yesterday. Real and affecting, it felt like warm sheets from the dryer.

And he was acting really weird. Warm sheets? It was a smile for God's sake.

But if she thought wearing those baggy slacks and a turtleneck made her smile less potent, she was wrong.

The library was a small brick building on the corner. It had been a long time since he'd been in one, but Lisa walked straight behind the desk like she'd been there hundreds of times. Probably she had.

"Hey, let me take that," a man's voice said from the stacks behind Joe.

Joe turned and found a well-dressed, preppy dude wearing glasses rushing to Lisa's aid. Probably Joe should have taken both boxes from the car. Why hadn't he thought of that? What kind of idiot lets a pretty girl carry a box of heavy books for a block without offering to help her?

The snappy dresser took the box from her and gestured to Joe. "Follow me, man." As Joe followed, he got an introduction. "I don't think we've met. I'm Adam Parker. Town librarian."

Adam dropped the box against a wall, so Joe put his on top and thrust out his hand. "Joe. I'm a friend of Ben Rhodes."

Adam's handshake was firm and sure. "Not the

Sergeant Carter we've heard about?"

"That's him," answered Lisa. "Joe is having Christmas with us, the poor guy. Which reminds me, my mom asked me to remind you you're invited to Christmas Eve dinner."

Joe watched the warm chitchat between the two and realized this Adam Parker would be the kind of guy Lisa should hook up with. Probably she already was. Parker was smart, friendly, and a good dresser...and they seemed to like each other well enough. He was intellectual, could probably talk to her about important things that Joe didn't know about.

Joe's gut churned, though he was going to blame that on too much breakfast and not jealousy. Because he had no rights to her. He wasn't staying and even if he were, she'd be better off with a librarian than a guy like Joe. Adam and Lisa fit together in a world that made sense.

But Joe never figured the world for making much sense.

If Adam and Lisa were dating, Joe had to wonder why she'd kissed him back when he'd laid one on her last night.

"Are you sure you won't change your mind?" she asked the librarian, obviously disappointed. He must have turned down the invitation while Joe was remembering how whiskey tasted off her soft lips and tongue.

Damn. What the hell was wrong with him?

"Plans this year with Simon, but thank your mom again for me."

"Will do." She looked to Joe. "What do you say, Joe? Think we have time for a hot chocolate before my brother finishes his shopping? My mom will be ecstatic if I fit in an unscheduled bonus Christmas activity." She turned to Adam. "I've never seen her like this. She's bordering on manic this year."

"I'm sure she's just glad to have your brother home." Adam smiled at her, and Joe wanted to punch something. He was never going to make it in civilian life if he didn't learn how to deal with people. But he really, really hated the idea of this librarian being perfect while Joe was anything but.

In the Army, Joe knew where he stood. In bars, he knew how to talk to women. How to get them to flirt with him. In any given situation, he was used to being in charge, respected. He did not like this lack of confidence he was suddenly feeling around a guy who wasn't even trying to size him up. In a physical fight, it was clear who would win, and that's pretty much how Joe was used to earning his place most of the time. The strong man, the confident man, wins. Wins the fight. Wins the pissing contest. Wins the girl.

But in Joe's new life, he wasn't sure if that was true anymore. Guys like Adam didn't have to be the alpha to get ahead in this world. Guys like Adam could date girls like Lisa and live in a small town and be happy around books and Christmas parties for children. And that was great. Really. He had no plans for Lisa other than being an extra brother for a week. That was it.

"I haven't had hot chocolate since I was twelve,

but sure, why not?" Joe inclined his head to Adam, searching the man's face for jealousy and found none. Idiot. Didn't he realize what he had? How easily he could lose it if Joe were a different kind of guy? The staying kind? "Nice meeting you, Adam."

Adam cocked his head, reading something into Joe's tone. *Good luck figuring it out, buddy. I don't even know why I'm upset right now.* "I'm sure I'll see you at the kids' party."

Joe and Lisa crossed the street to the coffee shop called Beans Crosby. Inside, the interior was like stepping into a vintage movie. Everything was gray and black and white with just a few punches of red here and there to draw the eye. The roasted beans smelled delicious, but he knew he was in for hot chocolate instead. Which was fine. Lisa tried to pay, and of course he didn't let her.

"Let's sit outside," she suggested.

"You'll freeze."

She patted her hat. "It's not that cold. C'mon."

They sat in front of the shop. The day was clear and crisp, but the forecast was calling for snow in the next few days. An honest to God white Christmas.

Lisa's cheeks flushed a pretty pink as she chatted at him happily about the town, the traditions, and her mother's crazy obsession with the perfect Christmas. He didn't have much to add, but he smiled while she talked, enjoying the stories and her animated expressions. So unlike the girl who blended into the scenery the day before. He liked that she was feeling comfortable with him again.

He realized, in a crystal moment of clarity, that

this was why he fought so far from home. So this girl with a pink nose could sip hot chocolate on a postcard-perfect small-town block. So others like her could enjoy the anticipation of snow and holiday cheer. He wasn't one of them yet, but a peaceful sensation stole over him thinking that maybe someday he would be. Could be.

And then she stopped talking abruptly and diverted her attention to her shoes. It wasn't until a man stopped in front of her, instead of going past into the shop, that Joe realized why.

His hackles were up and his muscles coiled in ready response.

"Lisa," the man said.

"Hello, Alan."

She didn't introduce Joe, but he wasn't offended. He realized something was very, very wrong and she was trying hard to hold it together.

"This your new boyfriend?" Alan asked, his face tight and lips curling into a sneer.

Lisa shrank further into her chair, so Joe stood, feeling at once protective and pissed off. He'd have liked to know why he was pissed, but it didn't matter. Not really. "I'm Joe. Friend of Ben's."

"You a soldier, too?" Alan asked. He was smaller than Joe, but he didn't seem too intimidated.

"Yeah," Joe answered. Because it was easier than using the entire explanation.

"Thank you for your service," he said, and it sounded earnest. Real. To Lisa, he added, "I hope you've done your service by telling him upfront about the kind of girl you really are."

Lisa's once pink cheeks were now ghostly white, and Joe had an urge to punch this Alan character.

"I think you better go on in and get your coffee," Joe growled. "If you continue to upset the lady, I'm not going to be happy."

"It's fine, Joe. I'm not upset."

Except he could hear in her tight voice that she was very, very upset.

"Let's see what kind of white horse you ride in on when you find out she's a liar. That she'll open her legs to anyone who asks."

Well, he'd warned him. Joe pulled his arm back and visualized how satisfying the crunch of Alan's nose was going to sound when a grip from behind stopped him from forward movement.

"This one's not worth your time, Sarge," came Roadie's steel voice. "Though I appreciate you looking out for my sister." Ben stepped in front of Joe and used his body to steer Alan away from Lisa. "Okay, Preacher Boy, it's time for you to hit the road and take all your peace, love, and joy with you. You know, I've seen a lot of really messed up dudes, but I've never seen one as judgmental and hypocritical as you. Because it's Christmas and I like your mom and dad so much, I'm not going to beat your pasty-white pansy-ass into the ground, but you talk to my sister again, and I won't be so gracious."

Alan shook his head in disgust. "You're not helping her by defending her, you know. She needs to come clean with the—"

Joe interrupted with a plea to Roadie, "Please, man. Just let me hit him once." Joe had no idea what this was even about, but he knew for certain he hated this Alan person.

"Please stop." Joe and Roadie both turned to the small voice. Lisa's eyes were rimmed with unshed tears. "Don't ruin Christmas. Let's just go."

They ushered her past the asshole. And into the car. When they got back to the house, she pleaded with them not to tell her mother, and she ran to her room.

"What the hell was that all about?" Joe asked Roadie as they moved into the living room, the fireplace like a magnet even though it wasn't that cold outside and they'd just come from a warm car.

"Not my story to tell, Sarge."

"I bet I could beat it out of Alan."

At that, Roadie smiled. "I wouldn't mind seeing that. He's a punk. I never liked him before, never thought he was good enough to date my sister, much less marry her."

"They were married?"

"No. Look, it's not my story."

Joe wanted to pull rank, but realized he couldn't do that anymore. "He made it sound like she—"

"My sister did nothing wrong. Don't even go there."

"I wasn't implying she did. I like your sister a lot. She's a nice girl."

When Roadie scowled at that, Joe wasn't sure what he'd said that made it worse.

Roadie shook his head and braced himself on the mantel. "Be careful about calling anyone a nice girl."

"Huh?" Last he heard being nice was a

compliment.

"Look, sometimes people put expectations on people. Put them in boxes and only allow for certain things. When you call a girl a nice girl, it's easy to forget she is human. Like the rest of us." He scrubbed a frustrated hand through his regulation short hair. "I've already said too much. Lisa would kill me if she knew I was talking about her. But just know that "nice girls do" or "nice girls don't" isn't something we like in this house."

And then he stormed out, leaving a very confused Joe and a crackling fire behind.

Chapter ★ Five

LISA HADN'T BEEN expecting the late-night knock on her door, but she was even more surprised to find Joe standing there with a bottle of whiskey and two snowmen mugs.

"You were quiet at dinner," he said. As if that explained his presence at midnight.

"I'm quiet a lot." He waited for her to invite him in, which she wasn't sure she wanted to do. "It's late."

"You don't owe me anything, Lisa, but I'd really like it if you told me what was going on with the asshole in front of the coffee shop today. I wanted to hit him. I still want to hit him."

"He's not worth it."

"You're right...but that's not stopping you from letting him get to you."

She wanted to send him away, except she didn't. She leaned her head against the door. "It doesn't concern you."

"Actually, yeah it does. I can't stand the thought of that weasel hurting your feelings. And he's going to keep doing it unless you stop giving him the power to."

That didn't explain why it concerned Joe, but she didn't want to chance someone coming up on him in the hall, so she pulled the door back and gestured him in.

He whistled as he turned a circle. "This is your room still?"

She laughed, taking in her Justin Timberlake poster and horse trophies and pink bedspread. "I don't live here anymore. I'm visiting just like you. But yeah...this was my room."

"This is actually kinda hot. I feel like I'm seventeen sneaking into a girl's room. Better fantasy than even the hotel bar we met at in the kitchen last night."

She unfolded her arms, knowing she looked like some weak shrinking violet when she hugged herself. "Well, you're the only boy I've ever had in here."

Their gazes clashed, and she felt his hunger. Hunger for her? Was it her or just the idea of sneaking into her teen room that had him hot and bothered? She grabbed a unicorn pillow off the bed and plopped onto the floor, her back against the bed, the pillow in her lap. "I bet you were a bad boy sneaking into girls' rooms all the time."

He joined her on the floor. "Maybe once or twice." He poured them each a drink. "Was Alan your boyfriend in high school?"

Well, he got right to the point, didn't he? "Yes."

"But he never came in here?"

She shook her head. "We didn't…we didn't have sex…not until prom." She shuddered thinking about the backseat of his parents' car. "And then it was just the one time. We'd been saving ourselves for marriage, but we screwed up once."

"Is that how you see it? Screwing up?"

"Alan was the son of a pastor. He wanted to be one, too. It was important to him that we do things the right way."

"But not you."

She shook her head. "Not really. I'm not religious. When was your first time?"

Joe squared his jaw and looked into his cup like he was hoping the answer was in there. "I was younger."

"How much younger?" The longer they kept the focus on him, the better she felt. She wondered what he'd been like as a teen. Trouble probably. He had that vibe.

"Probably too young. I don't…it wasn't great. I mean it was sex, so it was good, but the circumstances were less than ideal. I was too young. She was…I don't really want to talk about this."

Lisa snorted. Not very ladylike, but whatever. "Oh, but it's okay to talk about me and the weasel?"

He swallowed hard; his Adam's apple bobbed and she found it fascinating. "I lived in a foster home. A lot of different ones over the years. My guardian…she was lonely. I was thirteen."

All the blood leached from her face in a cold rush. "Oh, God. Joe..."

"Like I said. Less than ideal."

The idea of someone taking advantage of a young boy like that infuriated her. But he didn't come to her to rehash his own bad memories, so she changed the subject. "It might surprise you to know that my experience with Alan was also less than ideal."

This time he snorted. "Not surprised really. He seems..."

"He cried."

Joe spat the whiskey in his mouth back into the cup. "What?"

"He came, and then he cried. Told me we made a huge mistake. Wanted to pray right then and there for forgiveness. I had to push him off me." *Out of me.* He'd been still inside her when the sobbing had started.

"So you didn't..." The rest of the sentence was hanging in the air, unsaid but not unnoticed. *So you didn't come?*

Why this wasn't embarrassing, she didn't know. But talking to Joe felt natural. "I didn't. The tears were sort of a mood breaker." Not that she'd been close anyway.

"That's not why he said those things to you today, is it?"

"No. Are you sure you want to know all this?"

"Are you sure you want to tell me?"

"No," she answered. "I'm sure I *don't* want to. It's sordid and embarrassing."

Joe leaned back, resting his head on the mattress

behind them. "Did you cheat on him?"

"No."

"Then why... why is he so bent out of shape?"

Where to start? "I went to Florida for Spring Break with my sort-of-cousin Stella."

"She tried to give me a dog after dinner."

"Yeah, she does that." Stella had a way of matching stray pets to their new owners before they knew what hit them. "She's also a lot wilder than I am. More free. She always has been. Alan asked me not to go to Florida with her, but it was my last single girl trip before the wedding—we'd planned a June wedding after college graduation. So I went against his wishes." She'd never felt a sun like the Florida sun. So different from the Pacific Northwest. "One night, they were filming on the beach. We were curious thinking maybe we could be extras in a movie or something. Turns out it was the crew for *Wild and Crazy Girls* and ...we flashed the camera our boobs in exchange for a trucker hat." Her face burned with shame. "It wasn't even Stella's idea. It was mine. I wanted to do one thing that wasn't expected before I got married. I don't even know how to explain it."

A tattoo would have been so much easier.

"I think that's awesome. That's not what this is about? Did Alan find out?"

To hell with sipping, she chugged down the whiskey, enjoying the burn as it hollowed her out. "The weekend before the wedding, my bachelorette party crashed Alan's bachelor party. It wasn't like he would get a stripper or anything... we just figured a mixed party would be more fun. And it was. At first. We were all at Ironwing, the pub, not the 80s band, and one of Alan's roommates put in a movie."

"Oh shit."

"Yeah. Instead of hardcore porn, they popped in *Wild and Crazy Girls*, and Stella and I shot each other some freaked out looks. I mean, it would be too coincidental, wouldn't it?"

"Oh, mistletoe, it sure should have been."

"But apparently, Alan had a subscription. He got a DVD every month. My entire family was there...my brothers, my cousins, *my dad*. Everything happened in slow motion. The hooting and hollering died down until the room was quiet as a tomb. Everyone turned to stare at Stella and me. And then they turned their attention on Alan. He was furious. I'd never seen anyone so red. He just started spouting all these terrible things. Calling me names. Ben punched him once—he wanted to hit him more but my cousin the cop was also there, and he stopped him by threatening to take him to lockup. It was the worst night of my life, driving home with my father after that. But the next day wasn't any better. Alan insisted that I was a slut. A whore. And he told anyone who would listen all about it." Lisa took a deep breath, pushing the pain back down as it balled up in her throat. "I held out hope he would change his mind, but I finally canceled the wedding the day before we were supposed to get married."

"He's lower than a weasel."

Lisa shook her head. "No, he had every right to be mad."

"The hell he did." Joe's voice was low, his words sounding menacing. "That piece of garbage had no right to call you names that night, and he certainly had no right to them today. What the hell? It was *his* DVD. If he thought it was okay to watch girls flash their tits, then it shouldn't have made him mad that you did it. That's a fucking double standard."

Lisa shrugged. "It's different if it's your girlfriend, I think."

"Girlfriend? Yeah, it's different. You're *supposed* to love them unconditionally, not judge them for having the same feelings you do. Plus, he was ready to marry you. You were supposed to be his whole world, his life. You don't treat the best thing that ever happened to you like that."

Her family had told her the same thing, time and again. But it still felt raw. "You don't think I'm a —"

"No. I think you did something wild and crazy. I think you weren't taken advantage of—you knew what you were doing and it was your choice and good for you. I think the man who said he loved you should have stood by you. And I think tits are amazing. Nothing to be ashamed about, mistletoe."

The way he kept saying tits should have offended her, but instead, hers were responding. Perking up as if he'd called them by name.

She hugged the pillow tighter over her tank top and changed the subject. "It's your turn. Tell me something about you."

"What do you want to know? My life is pretty boring."

"I doubt that. But I want to know something

personal. I mean, I just laid out some pretty embarrassing stuff. You need to give me something."

"Something besides my first time?"

Lisa nodded.

Joe was quiet for what seemed like a long time, but was probably only a minute. He started and then stopped. "Nah. It's silly."

"Tell me."

His gaze went soft, like the lights were on, but Joe wasn't there for a minute. When he came back, he said very quietly, "I've never been hugged."

Chapter Six

HE'D NEVER SAID it aloud.
He never even gave much thought to the sentiment.

But now it was out there and he couldn't take it back and something squeezed around the emptiness where his heart was supposed to be.

"It's no big deal," he added quickly. But not quickly enough to stop the wave of pity that flashed over her face. Not quickly enough to erase the crinkle between her eyes. "Really. I don't even know why I said that."

"Joe—"

He pulled away. "Do. Not. Pity me."

She picked up his hand. Hers were small and soft. His were weathered and tough, probably causing abrasions on her delicate skin. "I don't pity you."

"Yes you do. I can see it. You're looking at me like I'm some kind of puppy you just found out in the rain. I don't need to be saved."

"Of course you don't. You're a good man."

He should get up. Leave her alone. Instead, he chuffed out a breath and concentrated on the way her skin felt against his hand. "I'm just a man, mistletoe. Nothing particularly good about me."

She twined her fingers with his. "I could go into the way you saved my brother's life, but you would say you were just doing your job. I could mention that your job was serving your country and that you've been honored and decorated for merit and service, but you would probably just say the Army was the only thing open to you anyway. So I'll just ask you to tell me."

"Tell you what?"

"Tell me how you got this far in life without..."

He closed his eyes because looking straight at her was not an option. Not now that she could see right into him all the way to his damn soul. Because she could and what if there was nothing there for her to see? "I haven't lacked for human touch. We've established that I'm not a monk."

Her voice came from far away, even though she was right next to him. Touching him. "Sex isn't what we're talking about, is it?"

He shook his head, swallowing the pride that urged him up and out of this room. This house. "I was three when they took me away from my mom. I had a lot of issues, but she had more. She hadn't been clean since before I was born, I guess. And it's possible that she hugged me and held me, but I don't remember it. And I suppose the first few foster families may have, but I don't remember them either. From the time I do remember, there was no hugging. There were some really nice people in and out of my life occasionally—they just didn't hold me. Which is fine. I'm fine. I don't even know why I told you."

"No girlfriend has just hugged you?"

She really didn't get it. Get him. "Lisa, I'm not the kind of guy who has girlfriends. I have sex with women I'm attracted to. Once or twice and then we move on. I don't stick. I don't know how to stick. I'm the kind of guy your brother should have known better than to let hang around his little sister."

She laughed a lyrical tinkle he'd like to hear again and again. "He's only ten minutes older than me. Ten minutes. And he thinks you walk on water. He's probably hoping you'd hang around me. He thinks I'm pathetic."

He opened his eyes at that. "He doesn't. Not at all. He thinks you're amazing. You *are* amazing."

She slanted her eyes away. "He wishes I was stronger. That I could let go of what happened."

Joe reached his free hand to her chin, gently inching her back to him. "You will. When you're ready."

Sitting on the floor of her childhood room, her chin in his hand, his other wrapped up in hers, was the most intimate he'd ever been with anyone. It wasn't like sex. Sex was bodies.

This, on her floor, was pulling him from someplace new. Someplace vulnerable and scary.

She was scarier than anything he'd faced in the

sandbox.

Those eyes lasered in on him. "You've never been hugged." He shook his head. "I can give you that."

The shock of absolute stillness anchored him to the impossible moment. To this impossible woman. Her words echoed in his head, reaching for dark corners and soothing the abandoned dreams of a young boy.

It shouldn't matter now. It didn't. He'd long ago come to terms with his childhood. Time made him a man. The Army made him a better one.

But he wasn't good enough for her. For this.

I can give you that.

It was too late to leave. Too late to turn her away. Because God help him, he wondered if she *could* give him that.

She pulled him down, anchoring his head to her chest. It was awkward. Like he was a child-giant and she was a too-small mother. He didn't know where to put his hands. He didn't know how to respond or how to relax.

This wasn't his choice, but turning away now would hurt her pride more than it helped his. He would do anything not to hurt her. Lisa shushed him as if quieting his mind, pressing him further into her until her heartbeat began to lull him. The rhythm steady, true. His hands found a place to rest on her body that didn't make him feel like a lecher. He willed the rest of his body to chill.

Lisa smelled good. Not like perfume. Not like a club or a bar, which often carried its scent onto the women he'd picked up in them. It wasn't even a scent he could place. It was just her skin.

In his life, women liked him for his body. He liked women for their bodies. He liked Lisa, and he'd admit he liked her body as much as if she were any other woman. But she wasn't. This was different. What she gave him, measured by heartbeats, was unlike anything he'd ever been offered before.

If Rhodes came in right now, he'd misunderstand. He'd think Joe was taking advantage—and maybe he was—but not like that. He wouldn't see that what his sister was giving Joe was more than a place to rest his head, more than skin and sensation.

It was connection.

And it was more dangerous to the both of them than if they were naked in the bed above them.

Chapter ★ Seven

THE DAY WAS bright—sunshine lit the kitchen in cheerful rays. Lisa slathered jam on her bread in short jabby strokes. Her mood not so cheerful.

Joe skipped breakfast in order to go for a run, which simply meant he didn't want to deal with looking at her over the cereal box. Because today was cereal and toast instead of the spread from yesterday. Mom was fighting a cold and went back to bed to get some rest. No big over-the-top breakfast today.

It wasn't like Lisa necessarily wanted to face him either. But at least she wasn't a coward about it.

Last night had been...hooboy. Like nothing she had words for.

What kind of woman offered to *hug* a man like Joe Carter? It had seemed like the right thing to do at the time, but now in the light of day, the super bright light of day, she wondered if she had been childish.

If Stella had a man like Joe in her arms, she would have hugged him, yes. But the evening would have ended naked.

Shame burned Lisa's face in splotches. Shame that she'd embarrassed them both. Shame that she wasn't woman enough to make love to a handsome man literally in her arms. Shame that she wanted to make love to him as much as she didn't.

"Today is bike day," her eldest brother said, reading off the itinerary on the fridge door, interrupting her thoughts.

Ben groaned.

"It'll be fun." She liked bike day. It was one of her favorite family traditions. And it would give her something to do to stay busy.

After cleaning the kitchen, the four Rhodes siblings and her dad trekked out to the detached shop. As the hum of fluorescent lighting started, she felt the jitter in her tummy. "How many this year, Dad?"

"Only ten," he answered and smacked a kiss on the top of her head.

"Ten?" Amy asked. "I only have an hour." She pointed to her chest. "The baby might not sleep on a schedule yet, but he sure does eat on one."

"So, you'll work for an hour. I think the rest of us can pick up your slack." This from Ben, who hated putting together bikes, but loved holding his nephew. Everyone did. The baby was three months old and already the sun of the entire family's universe.

They all went to work at their usual stations like elves in Santa's Workshop. And they pretty much were. Every year, they put together bikes for Toys for Tots. When they were younger, they each built one with help from their dad, taking a break midway for cocoa or a snowball fight. As they grew up, they got better and needed less supervision, but took more breaks—which led to the cell phone rule—not allowed in the shop—and adding more bikes.

At the hour shift change, her sister went inside to feed the baby, her dad went inside to check on Mom, and Ben asked their other brother to go give Joe a ride to Stone Rhodes to check on the Camaro so Ben could hang out with Lisa alone.

"What?" she asked as soon as everyone left. Surely it wasn't about Joe. He wouldn't have told Ben about last night.

"I just wanted to tell you that Nickelodeon is having a *Rugrats* marathon this afternoon."

She spun the wheel to make sure it didn't wobble while squinting at her brother. "You're a dork, but even you aren't that dorky. Why'd you get rid of Mal?" It's not like he wouldn't watch *Rugrats* with them. At Christmas they were all kids again.

"I just miss you."

She put down the WD-40. "I miss you too."

He pretended to be super interested in the bike chain in front of him because he was still a dude and dudes don't let their sisters see them tear up. Even dudes who were twins and their sisters already knew they were tearing up.

They didn't need words either, and for a few minutes, none were shared.

Ben broke the silence first. "So what do you think of Sarge?"

"He's nice."

"He's a good guy."

"Ben, you sound like Stella when she's about to give someone a dog. Stop it. Your friend has no interest in me. None."

Ben set his wrench down. "Because you dress like you're Amish."

She set her wrench down too—so she wouldn't throw it at his head. "Take that back."

"Can't. It's the truth. You can't hide forever."

"I don't like people noticing me. It's not a crime. The rest of you can have all the attention you want."

Ben popped up onto the workbench. "It's not working. Sarge notices you. He pretends not to, but anytime he thinks I'm not paying attention, he's watching you."

She picked up the wrench again for something to do. "You're making that up. Quit being a matchmaker; you're no good at it."

"Sarge is a good guy. You could do worse."

Must not hit brother with wrench. "Joe is a good guy, yes. He's also very good looking and doesn't need your help finding dates."

"So you think he is good looking?"

If a glare could melt his face... "Ben, stop. Of course he's good looking. But that doesn't mean he's a good match for me."

"You guys would have beautiful babies."

"Ben!"

"What?"

"If you want babies, go get a girlfriend and leave me out of it. I swear to God. Your ticking biological clock is not my problem."

"I don't want babies. That's why I want you to have them. I'm a much better uncle than I would be daddy."

That was categorically untrue, but she let it slide. "I love you, Benny, but I don't want to have babies with your sergeant."

"Ex-sergeant," came a voice from behind her. A very familiar voice.

Well, that's not embarrassing at all. She actually felt every color as it passed across her face. She must have looked like a kaleidoscope of pinks and reds.

"Ben, I'm glad you survived Afghanistan just to come home and be killed by your little sister," Lisa said, shooting him a look she hoped told him that she would get him back, and it would be spectacular. To Joe she said, "Hi."

His smirk held a thousand secrets. "Hi." He lifted his brows in a near waggle. "Sheriff Stone had a call, so he had to change our meeting to later today and your older brother is watching cartoons. I thought I'd come out here and help with the bikes."

Ben promptly gave up his station. "Here you go man. I'm going to go make some coffee, you guys want some?"

She nodded. She was going to kill him, but she might as well force him to bring her caffeine first.

"Sorry about all the awkward," she said when Ben

was out of earshot.

Joe just shook his head and picked up Ben's wrench. "I've put you in a weird spot with your family. It's my fault things are awkward."

"It's not. Ben is—"

"Right. He's right. I was standing there for a few minutes. I do...notice you. I can't seem to stop noticing. And that was before...last night."

Lisa pretended to be absorbed in the sprocket. "What do you mean you notice me?"

"Are you fishing for compliments?"

"What? No. I just mean...I'm not..." She looked down. "I don't stand out."

"Lisa?" She looked up and found him staring at her. She broke the eye contact, but he brought her chin back up. "You're beautiful. You stand out to me."

Why were there tears forming in her eyes? "I don't want to stand out."

He used his thumb to brush a tear off her cheek. "Are you sure? I feel like everything about you has been calling to me since I first saw you standing on the porch."

Her heart thumped a crazy bass rhythm. "Why, Joe? You could have anyone you want. Guys like you... I'm the friend of the girl you ask to dance. I'm never the girl."

He exhaled a harsh sound between a laugh and a groan. "Girls like you—hell, I've never met anyone like you before. You scare the hell out of me."

She wanted to ask why, but voices from outside carried into the building as her brothers and dad came back.

"Your mom is still feeling under the weather, so I'm going to take her to the doctor after we're done," Dad said. "You guys think we can get these bikes put together quickly?"

Ben handed her a coffee. "Good luck getting her to the doctor, Dad. She's going to fight you. It's a cliché that doctors make the worst patients for a reason." Ben squinted at Lisa, then used his napkin to blot the tear track on her cheek. He shot Joe a look, then brought his gaze back to her. She shook her head. It wasn't Joe's fault she had cried. She actually didn't even know what brought the tears on. But she didn't want him blamed for it.

She got to work on the bike again, trying to focus so she didn't obsess over the things Joe had said. What was wrong with her that she straddled the line between wanting to hide from men and desperately wanting Joe to find her worth looking for?

You're a slut.

No.

Logically, she knew she hadn't done anything wrong. It was Alan with the messed-up view about sexuality. But logic didn't help. Not when it mattered most. Not when everyone witnessed her humiliation.

It wasn't Alan who'd lifted his shirt for the camera. That was all on her, but why had she done it? Logic hadn't applied then either. At the time, it felt empowering, but that didn't make sense. How was it empowering to give men a look at her body, to view her as a sexual thing to be gawked at?

At the same time, it wasn't empowering to hide

her body, to be ashamed of wanting to enjoy sex. The one time she'd tried it certainly hadn't been empowering.

But where did that leave her now? Neither having sex nor hiding from sex had made her feel good, so where does a woman go from there? She wasn't a slut. Not in the hateful way Alan tried to imply. Wanting sex—wanting to be wanted—wasn't shameful. Why couldn't she get rid of his voice in her head?

She felt Joe's stare like a physical touch, but she ignored it. For now.

What would it be like to just pretend she was normal? While he was here, in town. He wasn't a forever guy. He wouldn't be here long, and he noticed her. Maybe it was only because she was some kind of challenge. He probably had women throwing themselves at him all the time, so of course the one who hangs back is going to get noticed. But she could use that, couldn't she? She didn't want forever. She was too screwed up to even think about forever. But replacing Alan as the last man who'd touched her wasn't a horrible idea.

She let her own gaze drift to Ben. He was pretending to build a bike, but he was intently watching Joe, concern etched on his forehead.

Ben wanted her to move forward with her life. He'd practically gift-wrapped Joe for her.

But Ben didn't know Joe the way she did. Would it be fair to use him to get over her lack of confidence? He'd already been used. Would that put her in the same category as the woman who'd taken his virginity?

That was icky. He deserved better.

Everyone would be better off if she went back to blending into the woodwork.

There. That settled that. Joe was only here for a few more days. She'd simply go back to being her normal, quiet self. He'd get the hint. He'd move on. She'd move on. Everything would be okay. She twisted the wrench one last time, making sure the bike was safe.

Being safe was important in this world.

Chapter Eight

SHE WAS HIDING from him.

Joe watched the way Lisa did it, noting when each of her family members noticed the withdrawal and when they decided to allow her the space. She had little tells. Quiet smiles that weren't real. The way she deftly turned conversations back to any subject that wasn't her. The way she found tiny chores that pulled her away but made her appear to still be present. The way she found pockets of solitude in a house full of people.

He wasn't the only one who noticed, but he'd bet she thought she had them all fooled. Her family loved her, worried about her, but didn't push her.

Joe really wanted to push her. He shouldn't have told her she scared him. It had made her pull back too much.

He respected her need for quiet. For solitude. But he resented the space she put between them. It was her right, of course, but he hated it. He hated that she thought she needed it. Hated that it wasn't even about him. It was about Alan.

Alan the weasel.

But what could he do? Spend the rest of his time in Silver Pines convincing her to move on from the weasel and then leave her just when she came around?

It had been almost forty-eight hours since they'd built the bikes. He hadn't been alone with her since. His time was coming to a close. He saw his car yesterday. It was almost done. A real beauty. Midnight blue with a white nose stripe. 454 under the hood and sitting on seventeen-inch chrome racing rims in the front and eighteen in the rear for a great muscle car stance.

And when her interior was done, he'd be on his way. Riding out of town like the Lone Ranger at the end of every episode. Better for having known Lisa.

Joe couldn't stop thinking about the night she'd hugged him. It had begun so awkwardly, but then something had changed. At least it had for him.

Was it platonic? Hell no. But it hadn't been a prelude to sex either. And touching her, being touched, fundamentally changed something inside him. A seismic shift.

But not the same for her.

She didn't want to see where this could go—because they both knew it could go nowhere. He'd been upfront with her about noticing her, and she'd stopped talking to him. Couldn't get more straightforward than that.

But that didn't stop his gut clenching because she was ignoring him.

After dinner, the family gathered around the television for yet another Christmas movie—this one a black and white deal. Joe was bored, but also entranced by watching this family interact with each other.

Amy's husband paused the movie so she could go put the baby down, and Joe's attention went straight to Lisa, like it always did.

"Mom, you look exhausted. Why don't you call it a night?" she said. There were deep lines furrowed over the bridge of her nose. Someday, some guy was going to have the right and the privilege to kiss them smooth.

"I can't. It is *Miracle on 34th Street* night."

Lisa sent a glance to Ben, and he picked up the argument. "Mom, we've all seen it a hundred times. You need to get some rest to knock out this bug. The kids' party is tomorrow. You don't want to miss that."

They got her to agree, though still not to see a doctor, and as soon as she left the room, Lisa announced she was driving into town to grab some things from her apartment.

"Take Joe with you," Ben suggested, to Joe's surprise. Roadie had never been stupid. Why would he trust a guy like Joe with his sister?

"I'm sure Joe has better things to do," she said, her cheeks pinkening.

He didn't have anything better to do, but that didn't explain why words were coming out of his mouth before he'd decided to say them. "I'd love to see the Christmas lights in town again."

Smooth.

She picked at likely nonexistent lint on her shirt. "You saw them the other night."

"But I want to see them again."

"Good, it's settled," Ben said. "Joe, that hat you wanted to borrow is in my room. You can come grab it and go."

Rhodes was not even trying to be subtle. He was going to have the big brother talk with Joe before they left. Which was good. But then Joe remembered the beautiful babies Rhodes wanted to saddle him with and started second guessing the drive to town.

Once inside Ben's room, Ben grabbed a hat off the desk and shoved it into Joe's chest. "You're one of the best guys I know, but you fuck with my sister and no one will find your body. Just so we are clear."

Joe couldn't have heard him right. "Excuse me? You're the one pushing me to go with her. It was your idea."

Ben folded his arms across his chest, his stance deceptively relaxed, but likely ready to spring into action. "You could be good for her. She could be good for you. But if you hurt her feelings like—"

"Do not say that weasel's name if you are about to put me in the same line-up."

"She told you about him?"

"Yeah. She told me."

The muscle in Ben's jaw ticked. "She let him into her head, man. It kills me that she hasn't been able to get him all the way out yet. I just don't want to push her from the frying pan into the fire. You have my permission to date her—"

"Dude, she would kick your ass if she heard you say that, and I'm tempted to do it for her. She doesn't need permission from you or anyone else—"

Ben narrowed his eyes. "Damn it, you know what I mean. Just don't hurt her."

"I'm not staying, Roadie. There's no reason for me to start something I can't finish."

"You could stay."

"And do what? There's nothing for me here."

Ben got quiet. "You don't have to start something. Just...just make her feel good about herself again. Give her some attention, you know? She needs to feel pretty and wanted again."

She didn't need that from a guy, she needed that from herself. But if Ben didn't get that, it wasn't up to Joe to explain it to him. "Permission to be excused?"

Ben shook his head. "Don't forget to wear the damn hat."

Chapter Nine

LISA PRESSED HERSELF against the back of her bedroom door, trying to get her breath back from her locked lungs.

Give her some attention, you know? She needs to feel pretty and wanted again.

Was it possible to die of utter mortification? Her brother felt he needed to coax his friend into giving her attention? The least he could have done was close the door. She'd been about to enter the room when she overheard them.

Pull yourself together, Lisa. She inhaled slowly until she got her lungs working properly again. She just had to power through this night. He could never know she'd heard that conversation. Never. She'd been through worse humiliation and lived to tell.

She just didn't want to do it again. God. Was she really so pathetic that her lot in life was just…shame?

A knock on the door jarred her and she squeaked.

"You ready to go, mistletoe?"

Damn him. Her nickname? Now? Really?

One more breath. In. Out. She opened the door, schooling her face into a bland expression.

"Yep."

She brushed past him, down the stairs, to the front door, ignoring Ben's goodbye.

She started her car and avoided the temptation to fill the awkward silence after he got in and buckled up.

Being a good hostess, she turned on the radio and strains of Alvin and the Chipmunks filled the car. Maybe not a great hostess because she left the station on, hiding her own wincing and tapping her fingers on the wheel as if she was enjoying it.

More awkward silence.

"Did you like high school?" Joe asked as they passed the schools.

"Yes."

"Were you in any sports?"

"No."

The next song came on. God, another one? Were they doing a chipmunk marathon?

She turned down a residential street that liked to do the light show up big, each house competing with the others on the block—each year getting a little nuttier.

"I bet you were a good student."

She shrugged.

"You're chatty tonight."

Breathe. In. Out. "I didn't invite you, Joe. You wanted to see the lights, but I didn't promise conversation."

Joe squared his jaw and twisted his head slowly. "Are you mad at me for something? You've been short with me for the last couple of days. And all these one word answers are getting a little old."

"I'm sorry I'm not entertaining enough for you."

He held his hands up. Oh good. That was universally as acceptable as trying to calm a person by telling them to calm down. "I don't expect you to entertain me. I just thought...never mind. I was wrong."

They didn't speak again until she reached her apartment downtown over the Ironwing pub. She jerked the car into park. "I'll be right out."

"Oh, no. I want to see your place."

"I don't think—" But he was already out of the car, waiting at the entrance.

She didn't have to go through the bar, so she led him up the stairs through her separate entrance, conscious that his eyes could be on her ass as she went up. But probably not. Her boxy jacket covered her butt anyway.

Maybe Stella would be home. Stella was good for distractions. Lisa enjoyed living across the hall from her because there was always something crazy about to happen in Stella's world. Living vicariously was as close to crazy as she wanted to get—but it was still entertaining.

Once inside her apartment, Lisa told Joe to stay in the living room while she got what she needed from her bedroom. Which was nothing. She'd only said she wanted to go home so she could have a break in her quiet space surrounded by her things.

Nervous sweat broke out, so she threw off her coat and picked out a new shirt. Another turtleneck. She stared at it. Hating it.

Her wardrobe was easy and modest. Neutral colors. Classic fabrics.

Boring.

She shopped in the parts of the store her mother refused to enter. She could trade clothes with her grandmother if she wanted to. She thought—she thought if she dressed the way she imagined a preacher's wife to dress, she would what…get Alan back? No. She had zero interest in getting him back. So why was she trying to be the girl he'd wanted her to be?

Now was not the time to analyze her wardrobe. She needed to get Sgt. Hottie out of her apartment. She wasn't going to get her break tonight. Wasn't going to sip a cup of tea from her favorite Wedgewood and curl up with her chenille throw. Was it too much to ask for an hour to decompress? She grabbed a duffel bag and stuffed it with some random things so she looked legit. Like she'd needed to come home. She was ridiculous.

"I think your apartment is amazing." His voice made her jump. He had to stop sneaking up on her.

She whirled around, clutching the duffel to her chest. "Amazing is kind of a strong word. It's a one bedroom above a bar."

He stepped into her bedroom. Uninvited.

"It feels like you. It's warm and I don't know…cozy I guess."

She snorted. He thought she was cozy. Basically, she was a twenty-five-year-old Angela Lansbury.

Fine. Maybe she was. And before he showed up, that was the way she liked it. Nothing wrong with Mrs. Potts.

"What the hell is your problem?" Joe crossed his impressive arms over his barrel chest. *Stop noticing his muscles.* He was all big and blocking the doorway and why couldn't he just go away so she could find her center again?

"I don't have a problem. Except for the big man in my bedroom swearing at me. I could do without that."

He took her duffel from her arms. "Don't even pretend you're intimidated by me. I want to know what changed. Something happened the day we built bikes."

Lisa pulled at her sleeves so they covered her hands. "Nothing happened. I'm giving you an out. Why won't you take it?"

The skin above his nose gathered in tight folds. Nice. Now there was a big man *frowning* in her doorway. Well, too bad.

"I don't understand why you think I want an out. I thought we were friends."

She'd thought so too. That's why she'd pulled back after the bike building—because she didn't want to use him to get over her insecurities. It was laughable now, her thinking she was doing him some kind of favor. He hadn't even wanted to be with her.

She tried to pull her bag out of his hands, but he didn't let go. "I don't want to be the reason you withdraw from everyone around you," he said. "Ever since I told you that you scare me, you've gone into your shell like a damned turtle."

She tugged harder on the bag. Turtle? "How long has my brother been convincing you to be nice to me? Was that the reason you came to Silver Pines in the first place? His poor little wounded sister needs a man to show her some attention? Just be nice to her, Joe...throw her a compliment here and there. How far does he want you to go? You really had me going there, the night you told me Ben wouldn't want you touching his little sister." She let go of the bag when it was clear he wouldn't.

She was egging him on—to what end she didn't know. But damn it, she wanted a reaction. Anger and embarrassment swilled together in her stomach like a batch of her cousin's moonshine. Potent. Wicked. Volatile.

But instead of sparking a similar rage in Joe, he dropped her bag on the floor. Calmly. Grr. Why was he so calm?

Without raising his voice, he asked, "Is that what you think? That he had to convince me to be nice to you?" His voice was measured. Too measured. That's how she knew he wasn't unaffected by the toxic brew inside her that seemed to spill out into the room. He felt it too, but Joe was not the guy who went red hot with rage. No, he went ice cold. "I guess you overheard him talking tonight?"

"I guess I did."

"This makes a little more sense then." He took a step toward her. Crowding her. "Don't back down from me."

She jutted her chin out. "I don't intend to."

"Good."

She'd never expressed anger at Alan. Not to anyone. She'd never felt she had a right to it. Not after what she did. But she felt angry now. Angry that she didn't know how to handle a man who showed interest in her. Angry that she wanted to go back to being a little mouse. Angry that she wasn't brave enough to do anything else. Angry that she couldn't trust that she hadn't mistaken interest for pity.

And logically, she knew it wasn't Joe's fault. Part of her felt like she should be tucking all the anger back in.

Part of her wanted him to see everything.

He pulled the hat off his head, clenching it in his fist near his thigh. "I told you things. Things I've never told another soul. Your brother has nothing to do with us."

"I heard him—"

"That was the first time he'd said anything like that to me. I hope you believe that. But even if you don't—you have to believe that night we had together."

Her brain tried to reject what he was saying. But she couldn't turn off what she'd felt. "Why?"

"Why did you brother ask me to be nice to you? Because he's worried about you. And he has no idea that I've already kissed you. That I've been in your bedroom. That I've felt closer to you than any other person in my entire life."

She closed her eyes, trying to block out the

conflicting emotions warring inside her. He could be lying. Covering. Trying to make her feel good. Just like Ben had asked him to.

His palm on her cheek made her open her eyes. "I'm going to kiss you again. And if you still feel any doubt that I'm here with you because I can't stay away, I'll walk out of this town and you never have to see me again."

He was going to kiss her? Every nerve ending in her body sang a hallelujah chorus. *No—Lisa, slow down. You don't want him to kiss you.*

Liar.

He just kept turning her world upside down until she didn't know what she knew or felt anymore. Could a kiss decide that for her? One kiss? It was one kiss that started this all. "What if I do believe you. What happens then?" What if he couldn't stay away? She wasn't ready for either proposition.

He moved his hand down, sliding to the back of her neck. "I have no idea. You ready to find out?"

Was she? Was she brave enough to just go with it, not knowing what came next?

She'd known all her next steps with Alan, and look how that turned out.

But she was angry and embarrassed and confused. Why did he even like her? How had he even seen her? The shadow she'd lived under since the bachelor party had cloaked her so well for so long.

Joe's dark gaze was zeroed in on her. He saw her. He knew her flaws, but he didn't turn away. Wasn't disgusted. She'd even been a shrew to him and still here he was.

She really wasn't ready, but she nodded.

"Not good enough. Tell me."

She rolled her eyes at him. She couldn't just *say* the words he wanted to hear. She wasn't like that.

He tugged on her hair, pulling her closer. Stared at her mouth, but didn't kiss her. He wouldn't be gentle, but he wouldn't push her.

And Joe would never cry while they were having sex.

"Kiss me, Joe. I want you to kiss me. And we'll find out what happens next."

Chapter Ten

THAT WAS ALL he needed.

He didn't want to waste time with soft, coaxing kisses. She needed to know how she affected him and his words weren't working.

He held her firmly, one hand wrapped in her braid, and slammed his mouth into hers. She opened for him instantly, allowing him to plunder with his tongue, his teeth, his lips. He needed to slow down, but he couldn't. This woman who pretended to be a mousy girl writhed against him, pulling him like the tide and he was powerless.

The rough demand of his mouth should have frightened her. It frightened the hell out of him. The kiss was against all rules of engagement. But more. He needed more.

Lisa unzipped his coat, pushing him away so she could pull it off his shoulders. He pulled her back as soon as she was done, burying his face in her neck.

Her gasped breath shocked the silence when he sucked on her earlobe.

"Oh God. That's so good."

His hands slid under her shirt, sweeping across the soft skin of her abdomen. She shivered when his fingertips grazed the bottom of her bra. Joe paused, pulling back to look at her face.

He wanted. God he wanted. He'd never let himself long for anything before. Not when he'd grown up knowing that it made you weak to need something you might not get.

But he wanted her. All of her. He wanted the taste of her on his lips. The slide of her skin under his hands. He wanted to bury himself inside her. And he could have all that right now.

But it wouldn't be enough.

He couldn't make do. He wanted her smiles. The light in her eyes. Her laughter and her tears and all the things he wasn't entitled to.

And most of all he wanted to erase her fear—the shame that warred on her face even now. He wanted to undo everything the weasel had said and done that had twisted her up inside. But he wasn't the one who could do that. Only Lisa could overcome that.

"Why did you stop kissing me?" she asked, and his heart broke at the dejection in her voice.

"I don't want you to regret me." He eased his hand out from under her shirt. "I want to take everything you offer, but I don't think I have enough to give you in return. But I especially don't want you to regret anything that happens between us."

Her gazed darted around the room like she just

realized where she was and what she was doing. She shook her arms out, shaking him out of her system.

"We've only known each other for what…four days?" She took a step back. Withdrawing. Every thought she had played across her face like a movie. "I don't want to be like this. I can't win. I know I can't. It's not wrong to want you. Why can't I get his awful words out of my head."

"Mistletoe, I want to swoop in like a knight in shining armor right now. I want to believe that I have the secret key to make you feel good again. That I could give you clarity through sex and that you'd come so hard and so many times that you'd never feel shy again." He laughed as she turned red. "And I am conceited enough to know I can make you come. And I might even be good for you." He eased back a step. "But it's not Alan that is slut shaming you in your head right now. It's you. And that I can't fix." He traced a finger down the curve of her cheek. "Only you can do that."

She blinked as if the room had suddenly grown bright. "You're…right."

"It happens once in a while."

"You kissed me like you want me. That's real, right? That's not some twisted—"

"If your brother knew the things I want to do to you, he'd lock you in a tower and me in a dungeon. I think you're amazing."

"You called me cozy."

"I called your apartment cozy. And believe me, that was the first time I'd ever said that word out loud."

She tilted her head, studying him. "You haven't had a lot of comfort in this life have you?"

"Not really, no."

"Is that something you want? Comfort?"

Joe thought he understood the lay of the land a few minutes ago, but she just flipped the map and everything was tilted and strange. He didn't know the answer to that. Was she trying to trick him? What did she want him to say?

Was she right? Was he looking for a cozy place to hide after all that he'd seen and done? Was he using her for something?

Or maybe comfort, the peace he felt with her, was what was telling him she was the one thing he was willing to yearn for after a lifetime of not allowing himself to want. She had him in knots. He ached in all the places she'd opened inside him. Ached for her.

"I just want you, Lisa."

She nodded though her concentration was elsewhere. Outside of the room. "I want to show you something."

Normally, that would trigger a most excellent response, but her expression made him wary. He followed her into the other room without saying a word. She stopped and opened a drawer, pulling out a DVD. Her hands shook.

"If that is what I think it is—"

Lisa straightened her spine. "It is. I want you to watch it."

"No. Why?"

She shrugged and opened the case. "I don't know."

Joe didn't know a lot of things, but he did know this was not a great idea. "Lisa—"

"I'm taking it back."

He didn't think she meant the DVD. "Taking what back?"

"My life."

Chapter Eleven

JOE DIDN'T UNDERSTAND and that was okay. He didn't need to.

She didn't understand it, though it was probably more important that she did.

Her hand trembled as she tried to place the DVD into the player. Trembled so badly she couldn't get it seated correctly. Joe stilled her with his quiet, warm fingers, taking the disc away from her and getting it into the machine. She backed up and used the remote to turn on the television.

She hadn't watched the movie since that night, but she knew where her cameo was thanks to Alan so thoughtfully including where to start when he'd mailed her the video. That wasn't all he'd said in the note, but she pushed those names aside and cued to the twelve-minute mark.

There they were. God she looked so young. It was hard to believe that was less than three years ago.

She and Stella answered a few questions—giggled mostly. Florida had been a blast—she just remembered that now for the first time. They done some drinking, sure, but they'd just laughed and laughed most of the trip. The booze hadn't been the highlight. The filming had just been a blip on her vacation until it came to symbolize everything about her.

But right there, at that moment, she'd been a girl having a wonderful vacation. That Lisa had thought this would be her secret forever. Something to remind her that she was capable of being surprising. Of having fun and being reckless.

Their intro was brief on camera. Lisa pulled in a deep breath. And then. Well. There *they* were. In all their glory.

The next segment came on before she realized she was off the screen. She paused the video and stole a look at Joe.

A shrug that pretended to be careless lifted his shoulder. "I'm not sure what you want me to say. Except that anytime you want to watch it again, I'm game."

A laugh escaped her, though it sounded more like a sob. The laugh had been acting like a cork and when it came out, it let out the stale air she'd been holding since the bachelor party. Pounds and pounds of air expelled into the atmosphere. "I do want to watch it again," she said. And she did.

They watched it two more times. Joe took the remote from her. "Well?"

He didn't call her names. He didn't act astonished

or disgusted. He didn't change at all.

She sank onto her couch. "I feel so light. So...free." Her face felt hot. "You probably think I am so weird right now. But did you see me? I had fun."

"Yeah, I saw you. Three times." He took the spot next to her. "For the record, that was insanely hot. Not just that you flashed the camera—but watching it with you. I know it was some sort of cathartic exercise for you, or maybe you meant to punish yourself or test me or whatever—but watching you flash your tits while standing next to you was damn erotic."

The turtleneck was too hot. "Stop saying tits, Joe."

"No." He picked up her hand. "How are you doing?"

"That movie was a stupid thing to do, but the stupider thing would have been marrying a man who judges girls so harshly while spending $29.99 a month to watch them." She knew it. She'd known it for a long time. But it wasn't until tonight that she finally knew it in her heart too, not just her mind.

"Thank God you dodged that bullet, yeah?" Joe sat back and settled her under his arm. "I don't want you to ever think badly of yourself. It doesn't matter if you do or don't have sex. Or do or don't wear tight sweaters. Or do or don't wear only shades of brown and browner." She pinched him. "The point is, the weasel and a lot of guys like him have two sets of standards for women, and neither is particularly flattering. You deserve better."

She rubbed her cheek against his flannel shirt.

She hadn't thought she'd find so much comfort with a man she hardly knew. But Joe was no weasel. "Thank you. For tonight. For...everything."

"I should be the one saying thank you." He kissed the top of her head. "We should go soon. Your family is going to wonder what happened to us."

The slap of rejection stung her already sore ego. He'd said it was erotic, but he wanted to leave? Kiss her on the head like she was a kid? She pulled back to a seated position. "You don't want to...of course not."

One sharp tug from Joe and she was in his lap. "Of course I want to." She felt how much he wanted to under her butt. "But not tonight. And I'll kick myself later for this. But tonight you're vulnerable and it wouldn't be right."

"I am not—"

He put a finger to her lips. "You are. But you won't always be. I want you to come to my bed with no regrets. The reasons we don't work haven't changed. I'm thirteen years older than you, and I'm just passing through. I don't have anything you need. Not long-term." He slid his hand up her arm and back down again, the heat of him searing her beneath her sleeve. He could make her feel too much. Maybe she didn't have the defenses for him just yet. "Give yourself a little time to make sure that's what you want. We don't have the future—but the present could be amazing."

He's as scared as you are. She didn't know a lot about men, but she was beginning to understand this one.

He was right—she was a little vulnerable tonight. She'd been dragging around chains so heavy Jacob Marley would have been proud.

But Joe wasn't exactly free of his past either.

"You told me once we were inevitable."

"I also told you I'm no good for you."

She pushed off his lap. "I don't need forever or long-term. I understand this is a fling."

He didn't correct her, so she went in the other room to grab her stuff.

She felt a tickle of the girl who wanted to do something unexpected. The girl she'd pushed down for the last few years. A fling with Joe was more dangerous than flashing her boobs on camera.

She really should think about just getting a tattoo.

Chapter Twelve

AFTER DELIVERING THE bikes to Toys for Tots, sledding on the mountain, and making curls out of ribbons for an hour—all three things he'd never done before—it was time to get ready for the kids' party. Joe been tasked with helping Mr. Rhodes...Mark...get the Santa suit on and get him to the party since he couldn't reach the steering wheel with his extra padding.

To say that it was unnerving to spend one-on-one time with the father of the woman he was currently trying to get into bed would be an understatement.

And so was the phrase "trying to get into bed." He'd had more than one chance to do so, and his body was currently hating him for discovering he had a nice-guy side. Joe was tense. Grouchy. And needed a release his morning run had not provided. If he didn't sleep with her soon, he was going to have to start a bar fight. He really didn't see any other way around it.

"How's your Camaro, son?" Mark asked while Joe attached his Santa belly.

"She's a beauty. Jason Rhodes should quit the sheriff gig and rebuild cars full time."

Mark laughed. "Not likely. He likes his job too much. What about you?"

Joe cinched the belt and hoped it would hold. That was more than a bowl full of jelly. "Me?"

"What are your plans now?"

He should know the answer to that. He wished he did. He was thirty-eight years old but he felt like a kid just graduating high school again. Not the kind of guy a man wants sniffing around his daughter, that's for sure.

"After the Camaro, I don't really know."

"Lots of men go into law enforcement after the military. Do you need to start working right away?"

Joe shook his head and helped Mark into the furry red jacket. "I didn't spend much over the years. My car is gonna cost me, but I have a good size savings. Plus retirement pay."

Mark nodded. "You should have Lisa go over finance stuff with you. She'll tell you she's just the bookkeeper for my parents, but she majored in finance. She could have gone anywhere. She's really good. But she likes it here in Silver Pines."

Joe smiled but didn't look up. He was sure the effect of hearing her name was written all over his face. He'd never had it like this for a woman before. A car maybe. A woman no. "Maybe I'll do that."

Mark sat in the chair, and Joe brought over the

boots. "You ever thought about teaching as a career, Joe?"

"Me? No. Why?"

"Ben tells me all the guys learned a lot from you. He thinks you have a knack for it. The patience he lacks."

The boot needed to be tugged. Hard. Mark grunted as it finally slipped over his ankle. "Sorry, man," Joe said. He got the other one on easier. "I don't have the education to be a teacher.

"There's the GI Bill."

"Who's going to let a man my age into college?"

"Lots of men your age go to college. Or change careers and go back to college."

Joe had never thought about that. Not even once. He'd never thought he was the schooling type. "If I ever went to school again for a job, it would be something for disadvantaged kids."

Mark hung his beard over his ears. "Really? Like foster kids?"

Suddenly self-conscious, Joe handed him the Santa hat. "I grew up in the system, so yeah." No shame, right? He'd worked hard to outrun the stigma, but it haunted him. Maybe it always would.

"We have a program in Washington you could volunteer for. It's called CASA. They train you to be guardian ad litem. I'll get you the brochure. You'd be a child advocate in the court system. It's a volunteer position—but the experience would maybe point you in the direction for a career."

Joe thought about that the whole drive into town. He'd never had an advocate for him when he was a kid. If he could do that for someone else...

"Hey Santa, do they have that program in other states too?"

Mark shrugged. "Probably. I'm only familiar with Washington laws though. It's a good state. You might like to stay. You know people here. There is a university twenty minutes away. Lisa could help you find a place in town."

Joe shot him a look, but Mark just chuckled, his stomach jiggling. "Ben told me you wanted to take Alan out with a punch the other day. That's a ringing endorsement as far as I'm concerned. My daughter could do worse."

"I'd still like one shot at his nose."

"I can't condone violence or breaking the law. But if you happened to find yourself in need of a lawyer..."

"I'll keep that in mind."

My daughter could do worse. Joe let that sink in the rest of the way to the community center.

At the party, Joe got swept up in helping Mrs. Rhodes and Adam the librarian for hours, but every sight he caught of Lisa stole his breath. She hadn't changed any on the outside—she wore a heavy, dark nearly shapeless skirt that came past her knees and her cardigan covered a blouse that buttoned all the way up her neck—but she shone the way the moon glints off snow. She could probably wear a nun's habit and he'd think she glowed. This was insane.

He and another man, Simon, were asked to move a heavy bench outside. Simon was hiding from Stella because she was trying to give him a three-legged cat, so they found something else heavy to move while they were out there. When they finished, Adam met them on the porch with two coffees and a flask. Simon bussed Adam's cheek with a kiss in thanks—and that's when it finally dawned on Joe that Adam was not in competition for Lisa. He and Simon were happy with each other.

The three of them hid out on the porch with the flask until Mrs. Rhodes came out for them. It was time to fold the tables and put the chairs away. He liked that she sought him out to help. He didn't mind hard work.

"Joe, thank you so much for helping tonight. I wish I felt worse about using my houseguest as the hired help."

"I like feeling useful, ma'am."

"I hope you also feel included. You fit in to the community so well tonight."

Joe added another chair to the stack. It was starting to feel like Mr. and Mrs. Rhodes were up to something. "Mrs. Rhodes, you know I can't—Mrs. Rhodes?" She'd turned an ashen shade and her eyes got glassy. "Are you okay?"

He thought she was going to answer, but instead her eyes closed and she started to fall. Joe rushed to her side, catching her mid-swoon and lowering to the floor with her. "I need help over here!"

Chapter Thirteen

LISA PACED THE too small waiting room of the ER. There were too many people in the small space. Too many voices. Too many questions. Unanswered ones.

And Joe. Walking toward her. Game face on. In control. He had her coat in his hands. "C'mon, let's go for a walk," he said, offering his hand.

"I can't. What if they come out to tell us something and I'm not here?"

"Your family will find you. They have this thing now where people can send messages to handheld devices. It's pretty cool, actually. I think I saw one in your purse. You can bring it with us."

Lisa sighed.

Joe stepped into her space and spoke low in her ear. "I've been watching you for a week now. I know the signs, and you need some space and fresh air. And probably a snack."

They were close. Sharing the same air. But she didn't move away. He radiated strength and she wanted to bask in it like a sun worshiper on a beach. "What signs? What are you talking about?"

"You get a look in your eye when you've had too much people time." When she scoffed, he squeezed her hand. "Baby, let me help you."

Well, if he was going to call her baby, she'd never be able to resist him. It didn't mean anything. It was just a nickname. Like mistletoe. But boy did she like it.

He slipped her coat onto her shoulders and her hand into his.

The night air was crisp and snow was falling. Some of the tension in her muscles lessened as soon as they got outside. He was right. She had needed to get out of there. But only for a few minutes.

"Tomorrow is Christmas Eve." She stopped, hit full force with all the thoughts that had been racing through her head since Mom collapsed at the end of the party. "What if my mom is really sick? What if this is her last Christmas? God. She can't be sick."

"Hey, hey, hey." He pulled her into his arms, his hands cupping her head protectively. "She's probably just got some kind of flu. Or she forgot to eat today. She's been feeling under the weather all week, right? I bet she just overdid it tonight trying to make the party special for the kids."

She clung to the lapels of his coat, anchored by him. "Thank you for catching her when she fainted."

"Well, she's not the first woman to swoon at my feet. I told you I was kind of a big deal."

She laughed. She actually laughed. Which only reminded her of how serious this night was. "Thanks for staying with us here tonight. I'm sure you're tired too."

"I don't have anywhere else I want to be right now."

He let go of her neck so she could look up. Their eyes met and his drifted to her mouth. Was he going to kiss her? Right now? Outside?

"Your lips are turning blue."

Oh. Guess not.

"We should go inside."

She nodded. "In just a minute, though, okay? This is nice. Being out here. With you."

He took the mittens that were flopping out of her pocket out and slipped them onto her hands. "This is the part where I get to say I told you so."

He took such care, smoothing the material, making sure they were tucked under her coat cuffs. He probably didn't know how well he took care of people. Where had he learned that in a childhood of not being held by anyone who loved him? "Are my lips still turning blue?"

"A little bit."

"Have any ideas how to warm them up?"

The dimpled popped out, making a rare showing. "I just might, actually."

"Lisa!" Ben's voice stopped her mid-swoon. She turned to the doors where he stood. "Dad's come out. He has news."

She slipped on a bit of slush coating the sidewalk in her haste to get back inside, but Joe caught her by the elbow and kept her upright. She'd need to remember to thank him. Later. After she knew.

God, what if it was really bad? Her mom was the center of all their lives. The idea of losing her...

"Stop expecting the worst," Joe said as the doors slid open.

How did he even know what she was thinking?

Then she saw her father surrounded by her family.

"Dad." She ran to his open arms. He was still wearing the Santa pants and suspenders, so out of place under the blinking fluorescent light. "Is she okay?"

"I'm going to tell everyone at once, okay, sweetheart?"

She nodded and folded herself into the ring of family gathered around him. Joe's hand found her shoulder, and she covered it with her own, grateful for his strength right now when hers felt in short supply. She tried reading her father's face. All she saw was tired.

"Sorry for the wait everyone," her dad began. "She's fine. She's going to be okay. We just needed a little time to process things before we could tell everyone."

Ben found her free hand and squeezed. It wasn't lost on her how much she needed the people in this room. How at this moment, she knew exactly where she fit. How she was scared, but not alone. Where their energy often depleted hers, in this moment her brothers and sisters and grandparents and Joe were the ones keeping her upright.

"Tell us what, Dad?"

Cancer. It had to be cancer. Her mom had been feeling off for days. Tired. Nauseous.

He scrubbed a hand over his face. "Your mom...well, there's no easy way to say this."

Her heart pitched down a cavern of sorrow.

"Your mom is pregnant. We're having a baby. Maybe two."

Chapter Fourteen

JOE CAUGHT HIS second swooning woman of the day when Lisa's legs collapsed from under her as Ben broke the awkwardly silent circle first to hug their dad.

"I gotcha, mistletoe."

Wow. Another baby. Maybe two. That meant Amy's baby would be older than his aunts or uncles.

Lisa straightened in Joe's arms. "I'm okay now, thanks."

But she didn't look so good. Joe's pulse sped up. Everything forgotten but Lisa. He pulled her back a couple feet from the crowd. "Your color is not great. Are you sure you're not going to faint? Maybe you should sit down. I can get a nurse or a doctor to check you out."

She shook her head. "I'm just...a baby? I don't even know how to react. I'm honestly just shocked."

"It's not good news?"

"No, no it is. It's not what I was expecting, but it is great. Greater than great. But, well, I'm sure there are complications to think of. She's fifty. But I'm happy. And I'm really happy she's not sick." She hiccupped a breath. "And I'm babbling. I feel like I just drank an entire pot of coffee."

He framed her face in his hands, cupping her cheeks gently. Searching for what? How would he know if she was okay? He wasn't a doctor.

Her eyes were clear and shining with unshed tears. Her face regained its color. And then she gave him a lopsided smile. Everything inside him unraveled while he looked into her eyes. He'd meant to comfort her. To help her deal with the shock and the fear, but his emotions were unspooling wildly. He'd lost all slack on the line to his heart.

She didn't pull away. Didn't close her eyes as he brushed his lips softly over hers in a hospital waiting room filled with her family. He scraped his teeth lightly over her bottom lip and she closed her eyes then and let out a little purr of pleasure. He wanted to tip her head back, deepen this kiss. But no, not here. Not now. He let her go.

Dazed, she joined the rest of the mob around her dad. Mrs. Rhodes would be staying in the hospital overnight. No, they hadn't done an ultrasound to see if there were two in there, but it was a real possibility given that she'd given birth to two sets of twins and the Doppler seemed to detect a second heartbeat. No, they hadn't been planning or trying for another, but yes, once the shock wore off they were both happy. Nervous but happy.

And he wanted them all to go home. He'd bring their mom home tomorrow after the ultrasound, but she gave strict orders that they were not to hang out in the hospital all night. She was fine. This was just a precaution.

The siblings scattered after Mr. Rhodes returned to his wife. Since their mother wouldn't know, Amy, Mal, and Lisa all wanted to go to their own homes for the night and meet back at the parents' in the morning. Without a single excuse that made sense, Ben got Joe to take Lisa home. Even though she had her own car. Even though someone would have to take her car to her in the morning. It was a set-up. When Lisa didn't fight it, Joe decided not to either.

"Walk me up?" she asked when he pulled in front of her building.

And this was it, wasn't it? The inevitable he'd been trying to put off?

"Is that what you want?"

"I asked, didn't I?"

"Well, I wouldn't want anything bad to happen to you from here to your apartment."

His heart thudded loudly in his ears as he followed her in. She unbuttoned her coat and pulled the chain on an old-fashioned lamp. The warm glow from its leaded-glass pattern caught all the different shades of her hair.

...inevitable. The word echoed in his head, mocking him. Encouraging him.

She threw her coat onto a chair and stretched her head to one side, elongating the neck he'd like to spend hours on.

...inevitable.

She rolled her aching shoulders back, lifting her pert breasts in their prim blouse and cardigan.

...inevitable.

Who was he to fight it? If she'd have him, he was hers. At least for tonight.

But only for tonight.

The weight lifted off him. He'd probably already fallen in love with her. There was no way around that. But she would be more careful with her heart. He'd leave town before she gave it to him. They'd have this night. Then she could move on from the shadow she'd been hiding in. Find the guy that was right for her. Smart like her. Knew how to stay.

"You can stay," she nearly echoed his thoughts. "If you want." She fidgeted with her sleeves, pulling them down like she preferred them, so that only her fingertips poked out.

"I do."

He shrugged off his own coat, watching her watching him. She didn't seem frightened, but he wanted her to be sure. Sure she was ready. Sure she understood what he could and couldn't give her. He moved slowly, dropping his jacket on the same chair she put hers.

She reached for him first. An innocent caress from his temple to his cheek that damned him forever to a longing he knew time would not erase. She'd move on, but he had a feeling he never would.

She unbuttoned her cardigan with trembling fingers, eying him warily. As if daring him to react.

The blouse came next. Slowly, God so slowly, she

undid the buttons. The scant inch of skin exposed by the two pieces made him harder than any lacy lingerie or tight mini-skirt ever could. She pressed her lips together, tension tightening her features, going someplace else mentally. As she was about to separate the blouse from her body, he told her to stop.

He wanted all her attention to stay right here. In this room.

"Just wait," he said as he crossed behind her and undid her hair from the elastic band that held her braid. Fingering through the golden waves, he felt the relaxed sigh of her muscles as she eased closer to him. He wrapped his arms around her, pulling her all the way to his chest and resting his chin on her shoulder. Holding her, just holding her. He committed the moment to memory. The way she melted into him. The fresh linen smell of her. Even the way he hurt with wanting her so much.

He nuzzled her neck, remembering how much she'd liked it last night when he'd taken her earlobe in his mouth. When he repeated the move, she squirmed against him, shuddering with pleasure. Feeding his own.

It was *his* hands that removed her blouse as she came alive under his caresses with little quivers. All the things she'd been hiding so deeply inside her rising to the surface. For him. Pushing her hair over her shoulder, he nipped and licked a trail up and down her spine, pausing briefly to unfasten the bra that kept getting in his way. She stiffened for a second, but relaxed again by the time it hit the floor.

He tried to stop thinking of her breasts, the way he'd seen them on the screen last night. Tried and failed. He really wanted to see them again but worried his reaction might damage the ground they'd gained.

It dawned on him just how much responsibility he had tonight. All the ways he could screw it up. A hot ball of panic rose in his throat, but he swallowed it down, fire and all. What she needed was a man. A confident lover to erase the touch of her last. He would be that man or he would die trying.

He spun her around and latched on to one breast using his whole mouth, his tongue, his teeth as he walked them to the wall so she had some support. She was going to need it. He intended to turn every muscle she had to jelly.

She arched and cried out, first maybe in shock, but then in a desperate keening sound he'd hear long after this night was gone. Her fingers grasped his shirt like a lifeline as he drove her on and on with his mouth. Her breasts were perfect. Better in person. And that they'd been in protective custody for so long was a crime. She was sensitive, more so on the left, so he spent a lot of time there.

Desire clawed him inside like a feral beast. He was sure they were both going to come just from him sucking on her breast.

He picked up her hands and pinned them against the wall on either side of her head. "I just want to look at you." For both of them, she needed to be okay with that.

She nodded and he touched her with his eyes. The milk-pale skin, red where he'd scraped with his teeth. The rose-tipped nipples, proudly hardened with desire. The freckles that dotted her chest. Joe didn't know much about art, but he knew it when he saw it.

"You are so beautiful."

"Joe..." She paused. "I want to feel you. Your skin."

Done. He needed it too. To have nothing separate them. Flesh to flesh. He took his hands off her long enough to reach back and pull his flannel and undershirt over his head.

She wrapped her arms around him, holding him tightly to her. Her heart drumming against his.

He was lost to her now.

His hands skimmed the column of her waist and his mouth took hers hotly. She began to move instinctively against him, her breasts crushed between them. Nothing in this life had prepared him for this. For the feelings coursing through him like blood. He wanted to protect her, and at the same time, devour her. There was nothing safe about love. Not for him. Not for her. He knew that now.

Her skirt and panties got pushed down, and he followed them, dotting her body with kisses as he went. He murmured words of a lover against her stomach, her hip, the top of her thigh. She tensed when he kissed her in the soft curls of her sex, but went lax as he drew all her passion to one blissful point on her body. She didn't take long to climax, and he watched her face as the pleasure overtook her. Her shock. Her smile. Her surprise when it started rising again.

She was tight around his fingers. The weight of responsibility hit him again as he realized she was nearly a virgin. It might be painful for her if he didn't take care. And so he worshiped her for a long time. When he carried her to her bedroom, she was boneless in his arms. He settled her on the bed and wondered if he might have to let her nap first, but as soon as she heard the rustle of his pants she sat up, watching intently. Eagerly. He raised his brows.

"I'm only shy about my body, not yours," she explained wearing a smile he hadn't seen before. One he put on her face. "I want to touch all of you."

"Oh really?" She didn't look so shy right now, thank God. She wasn't covering up. Wasn't turning pink. Wasn't doing anything but waiting for him to finish taking off his underwear. And her unabashed words pushed his passion for her higher. To the breaking point.

And then she got tired of waiting and crawled to the end of the bed, got up on her knees, and without taking her eyes off of his, lowered his shorts. "Really."

She touched him with wonder. Laughed at his harsh hiss of pleasure. He wouldn't last, not like this. Not with her caresses and the way she scraped her nails along his skin when she took him into her mouth. So he threaded his fingers through that golden hair and pulled her back up, kissing her until she was breathless. Until she fell back on the bed with him above her, until he pulled away briefly to put on the condom.

Her body yielded so sweetly to him. His heart did

the same for her He'd never loved anyone. Never used his heart. Never thought it even worked. But he loved now.

She came again, crying out his name, and he let go. Let the primal beat overtake him. Let his heart open fully. Let the world collapse and obliterate all that was old and unwanted.

He shook with the need to tell her. To make her understand. But he wasn't that brave.

Now that he knew all he'd been missing, how would he ever let her go after tonight?

And tonight was all he had.

"Joe?" She broke the silence.

"Yes."

"You're leaving me tomorrow, aren't you?"

How did she even know what he was thinking?

"Yes. I think it's best. I don't... I'm not staying in Silver Pines. It would be wrong for me to lead you on."

She bristled and pulled out of his embrace. "I'm a big girl. I know I've had some issues, but I'm not naive. I don't need to be protected."

He rolled to his side to look at her. "I'm not trying to be an asshole. The longer we hang on, the more it will hurt. But I don't want you comparing me to—"

"Don't." She sat up. "Don't bring him in here and ruin this for us. I always knew you would leave. You never told me you would stay. And I wouldn't have had sex with you if I thought you were."

Well, now he knew exactly what an icepick to the heart felt like. "You wouldn't have had sex with me if I was staying?"

"No. You helped me because you were just what I needed. A temporary lover. Someone who cared about me and respected me, but someone who isn't part of my life. Who didn't know who I was before that night. Someone who won't know what I become after this one. So don't patronize me with your fears of leading me on. I didn't *let* you make love to me to get me over my fears. I *chose* you."

God, he loved her.

He sat up too. "I'm sorry. I'm not good at this. I didn't mean to sound patronizing."

"You should stay through Christmas."

Every day he stayed would make it that much harder to leave. "I need to go find out who I am when I'm not Sarge."

She nodded. "But you'll stay tonight."

"You sure you want me to? I don't want you to feel like I'm using you. That all I wanted was—"

"I thought we just established that I was using you for sex. Let's get under the covers though because I'm freezing."

Chapter ★ Fifteen

JOE WAS GONE when she woke up.

She'd known, as she'd fallen asleep, that he would go.

Her heart ached unpleasantly, but he'd given her so much more than he'd taken.

He was scared. She understood. He'd taken a lot on in the past week. Going from a loner to the thick of a large family Christmas. The drama of her parents. The drama of her insecurities. It was enough to overload anyone, and he also had his own big changes to think about.

But a note would have been nice.

She wanted to be pragmatic about it. Many women have one-night stands or short-term relationships. You don't have to be in love or in a committed relationship to have sex. Good sex. Fantastic sex. But she wasn't pragmatic. And her heart was already in the game. And while she wouldn't trade this last week with him for anything in the world, she still wished he had stayed. Had wanted to stay.

Even though she'd told him differently.

She knocked on Stella's door way too early, but she couldn't wait any longer.

Stella answered, blurry eyed but holding a cup of coffee so at least she hadn't woken her. "What's up? Merry—" Then she really looked. "Oh honey. What's wrong? Is it your mom? Come in, come in."

Stella pushed Lisa gently onto the couch, covered her in a blanket, and walked across the room to the kitchen to pour more coffee. She came back with the mug half full and a bottle of Irish cream, with which she liberally topped off both their mugs.

Sitting cross-legged on the couch next to her, Stella listened to Lisa's whole story. Showing surprise only when she got to the part about showing him the DVD.

"Why would you do that?"

"I don't know. Why do people get on airplanes to get over their fear of flying?" Lisa poured more "creamer" into her cup. "I needed to see how he would react. How I would react. It was only scary until I did it."

"And you guys had sex and it was great and then he ran away?"

Lisa nodded. "But here's the crazy part. I think he'll be back."

There. She said it out loud. She didn't want a temporary lover like she'd babbled about last night. She wanted Joe. She wanted a real relationship. And her heart, the wretched thing, was convinced deep down inside, he wanted that with her too.

Stella frowned. Contemplated her empty cup. Frowned some more. "Some guys just aren't the sticking kind, sweetie. I mean, I hope you're right, but maybe you should prepare yourself for that not working out the way you hope." No longer satisfied with an empty mug, she got up, grabbed Lisa's cup, and brought them both to the kitchen for a refill. "You know that saying about how people come into your life for a reason or a season? Or something? Maybe his entire purpose was to bone you and get you back on the horse."

"Stella!"

"What?" She handed her the coffee. "Honey, it was time."

Well, okay. She wasn't wrong.

"Besides," Stella went on. "You could not have picked a better guy to get you over the hump."

"I never noticed how many clichés you use before you've had enough coffee."

"Ha-ha. But seriously. He's older and has more experience than you. He's way hot. And he's a nice guy. Even if he isn't the sticking around kind—he's a nice guy. He's a war hero. He spent oodles of money at my brother's shop which means I better get a good Christmas gift with all Jason's extra money. And he almost took a dog. Thus, he was perfect for re-wetting your whistle."

"Seriously, Stella. Either drink your coffee faster or stop adding the booze. I'm going to make you give me a quarter for every cliché from now on." Lisa took a deep breath. "But thank you. I feel better. You'll be at dinner tonight, right?"

"Of course. You said you mom is okay, but are you sure she's up for the big dinner?"

"Yeah, about that." Lisa hadn't even had a chance to really process everything yet. "You know how my mom told us the other day she was going through early menopause and we kind of changed the subject because she tends to overshare when she starts talking about medical stuff?"

"Yeah."

"The very esteemed Dr. Rhodes completely misdiagnosed herself. She is not going through the change—well, not that one. And she does not have a touch of the flu. She's pregnant."

"Oh my God. Your mom is going to have a baby?"

Lisa nodded. It felt so weird to say it.

"Your mom is going to have a baby before we do."

"Stell, we don't even have boyfriends. I think we're doomed."

Stella sat back. "Frankly, I think your mom is doomed. I'm pretty sure having a baby at fifty is a lot harder than having one in your twenties."

"Do you want babies?"

She took a little too long to answer. "Yeah. I think so. Maybe. Someday. But I've already decided next year is the Year of Stella. No boys. I'm just going to concentrate on myself."

Probably a good thing. Stella's ex was only marginally better than Alan the weasel.

"A week ago, I didn't think I would say yes to someday. I didn't think I ever wanted to let another man close enough to get in my head, you know? But now—now I can see it. Someday. Maybe."

So he'd given her that at least. He'd given her "maybe someday" back.

Christmas Eve dinner without Mom at the helm had been different, but they all worked together, taking turns keeping Mom in the recliner when she tried to help.

Ben said absolutely zero about Joe all day. She hoped that she hadn't made their friendship weird. Joe didn't have a lot of friends. She didn't want him to lose Ben.

In fact, nobody said anything at all about Joe. It was as if he'd never been there. But he had. She ached for him, wishing she knew where he was. Then getting mad at herself about it.

She hadn't figured him to be the kind to leave without saying goodbye. Not after everything they'd shared. Which is why she probably got sadder as the evening went on. She'd really thought he'd come back.

She was getting figgy with it in the kitchen, pulling out the fig pudding for the carolers, when Stella's sister Megan came in to see if she needed help.

"Nah, I don't want you to hurt your new engagement ring. Were you expecting a proposal tonight? You looked pretty surprised." The entire room had hushed as he got down on one knee in front of the decorated tree.

Megan blushed prettily. Megan did everything prettily. "Brad and I have talked about getting married, but I wasn't expecting this tonight." She held the ring up to the light. "He really surprised me."

"Well, it was sweet."

"That's my Brad."

Lisa considered the pudding cups carefully, though her mind was not on pudding. "How do you know when it's love? When it's real? I thought I knew, three years ago, but I was so wrong."

Megan put her hand over Lisa's. "I'm sure Stella would tell you differently, but for me, Brad was right on paper before he was right in my heart. I know she's all about grand love and heart racing—but for me it was a slower fall. I dated Brad because Brad was the kind of man I wanted to marry someday. I was very logical about it."

"But you did fall?"

"I'm still falling. Brad is wonderful. I'm no help, am I? I don't know how you know. You just do. Sometimes the one that looks good on paper is the one—sometimes not. I mean, look at our parents."

In another world, Lisa's father and Stella, Megan, and Jason's mother were going to get married. Which is how they ended up almost cousins. And on paper, sure, they'd have been a good match. But their hearts knew differently. Her dad met her mom shortly after Stella's mom left him at the altar.

Lisa and Alan had been a good match on paper also. Until the match struck and burned the paper to a crisp.

Gah. Why was love so complicated?

She wished Joe were here tonight, but what would she say to him if he were? It was too soon for *I love you*. It was too soon for *Stay*.

And now it was too late for anything at all.

Her dad popped his head into the kitchen. "Ah, pumpkin? There's someone here to see you. We tried to send him away, but he insists he just wants to apologize, so …"

She brushed past her dad and ran into the great room. She knew it. He couldn't leave without saying goodbye. Maybe he couldn't leave at all. If he wanted to—

She stopped as if a door slammed in front of her. "Alan?"

Surrounded by every male in her family, Alan looked to be several inches shorter than she remembered him being. He wore the same ugly Christmas sweater he'd had since college. At the time, it had been cute because to Alan, it wasn't ugly. He'd liked the green with white trees and antlers. He wore it in the spirit his grandmother had knit it for him. Now that shade of green made her see red.

He held his hands out to the side in a plea. "Can we talk?"

Stella put her arm around Lisa. "I don't think so, preacher boy."

Lisa watched his face. Daring him to say something. She might be ready to be angry now. And she wasn't a slut. She wasn't a whore. It was time she faced him without the shame. His usual sneer was missing. He wouldn't have come this far up the mountain to insult her. Something else was going on.

She didn't think her family knew how to be this quiet as the only sound in the room came from the grandfather clock in the corner, counting down the seconds until she answered him. "Sure. Join me in the kitchen."

Stella didn't let go. "Not a good idea, babe. He's toxic."

She shrugged. "It's Christmas." And she was immune to his poison now. At least, she hoped she was. Mostly immune, at least, right?

Her dad stopped her halfway, allowing Alan to go in ahead of her. "I'd feel better if you brought someone in there with you."

She hugged him. Kissed his cheek. "I'm fine, Daddy."

"I'm not worried about you. I'm worried about him." At her quizzical expression, he added, "There are lot of sharp things in the kitchen, pumpkin. Keep in mind that I'm a lawyer, but I'm not a miracle worker. There are too many witnesses in here to make a self-defense case."

"I'll keep that in mind, counselor."

She paused to hug him one more time. Not once had her dad ever let her down. He'd never had a sharp word for her about the stupid DVD, the failed wedding that he and her mom had spent so much on, or for her inability to grab her life back after the humiliation she brought to their entire family. He'd just stood in her corner, waiting for her to need him. Her dad, her family, was really amazing. "I love you,

Daddy."

"Love you too, pumpkin."

Once in the kitchen, she forced herself to keep her eyes on Alan's face and not her shoes. She was done with looking at her shoes.

He put on his pastor smile. "Thank you for seeing me."

She didn't smile back. "Why are you here?"

This time, he looked at his own shoes. "I want to apologize. I know it's too little too late, but I wanted to tell you that I'm sorry."

"For what?"

Oh, the look on his face was worth letting him in the house for. Did he think this was going to be easy? That she would let this be easy for him? "For the things I've said," he answered matter of factly

"I see." She went back to her figgy pudding, knowing of course nobody would eat it. The carolers would take it, but they wouldn't eat it. "You're sorry for the things you said. The things you said last week at Beans Crosby? Or the things at your bachelor party? Maybe you mean the months after? Are you sorry for not offering to pay my parents back for half the money they spent on deposits for the wedding you canceled? Are you sorry for telling me you loved me, but treating me like a piece of trash the next day?"

She loved him once. That's what hurt the most. He stood in front of her now and she remembered what it was like to be in love with him. And she remembered what it was like to be betrayed by him.

"I'm sorry that I called you names. I'm sorry for

the way I treated you then and recently. The money part hadn't occurred to me until you said it just now—but yes, of course I should pay my half."

She slammed the wooden spoon down. "Why are you here? Why now? Just in the last week you called me a whore in front of my brother."

"This isn't easy for me, you know."

Lisa crossed her arms over her chest. Did he think she was going to fawn all over him? She glanced at the butcher block where the knives were. Alan took a step back.

"Are you here for my forgiveness?"

"I wouldn't turn it down. But I'm here for myself." He walked to the window—whether to get further away from the knives or just to think, she didn't know. "I told a friend of mine that I saw you the other day. I was up on my high horse, thinking how much better I was than you, when she told me that the anger I felt was at myself not you." He turned back to her. "I thought she was nuts until I realized she was right. Not right away. First I was mad at her for being right. That's how I do things. I get mad at other people instead of myself. I blamed you that night because I was angry at myself for owning that movie. I blamed you when we went too far on prom night. I blamed you for a long time that my life was off plan— that you took me off my trajectory, when I was the one who did that."

Lisa plopped onto a stool. Ugh. He was making sense. It was hard to hold on to the bad feelings when he was making sense. "You were mad at me because you were human you mean?"

"Because I'm a hypocrite."

The word hung in the room, heavy and full.

"I'm just a man. Not always a good one, despite the fact that I think I am always right. And I'm sorry. So, I'm here tonight, laying my ego down because I want to be the man God wants me to be. I'm still a jerk a lot of the time, but I'm trying to get better. My faith is important to me, Lisa."

She didn't want to, but she believed him. He really did have faith. He really did want to be a pastor, a good one. And it took guts to admit he hurt her because he was selfish.

He was human. And humans made mistakes. She'd made some too—but not the ones she'd been self-flagellating herself about the last few years. And it was time to come clean there as well. "Well, I'm sorry too, I guess. I never wanted to be a preacher's wife. I would have made a horrible one. I was always trying to act the part, but I was only showing you what I wanted you to see."

She'd been playing a role. It was so much better for them both that they broke up before the wedding. She wasn't even religious. What had she been thinking?

He nodded. Accepting her apology in a way that made her think he might even be a *good* pastor someday. Maybe he'd grown up, too. "Whenever I think about that night, I get angry. And that is always going to be a problem I need to work on. But I'm also very angry that I've said the terrible things to you. I'll have to live with that." His fingers traced the pattern in the granite counter top. "I know we won't ever be friends again. And I know I'm always going to fight with this ego I have. But I wanted to tell you I'm sorry and I hope that offers you some kind of benefit." He straightened. "With that I wish you and your family a Merry Christmas."

She nodded and another chain loosened.

She wished she could tell Joe.

"Merry Christmas." They wouldn't ever be friends again. That much was true. But letting go of the hurt would have to be enough.

Movement outside the French doors caught her eye. The carolers had arrived. She crossed the room to open the doors.

"Silent night..."

"What the fuck is going on in here?"

Startled, Lisa and Alan turned to the other door and the very upset Santa Claus standing inside of it.

"*Holy night...*"

Wait. Santa?

"Santa?" Alan echoed her thoughts.

Chapter Sixteen

SERIOUSLY, WHAT THE fuck?

"All is calm..."

Joe fought every urge to rush into the room and pummel the weasel into the ground. Alan was lucky that every pound of padding in this ridiculous red suit slowed Joe's progress across the kitchen, as well as Stella pulling on his arm from behind him.

"All is bright..."

"Relax, St. Nicholas. This is my fault, I should have given you a little more warning about what you'd find when I told you she was in the kitchen," Stella said, yanking on him.

"...tender and mild..."

His eyes met Lisa's across the room. Her very surprised eyes. "Joe?"

He stopped fighting Stella and stood in place, dropping his Santa bag at his feet. He cleared his throat. "Um. Ho ho ho?"

The rest of the family filtered in to listen to the carolers.

"Joe?" she repeated. "What are you doing here? Why are you dressed like Santa?"

He'd get to that later. "What am I doing here? What is *he* doing here?" He pointed at the weasel. "Aw, hell." With that he finished crossing the room and punched him square in the nose, the sound just as satisfying as he imagined it would be.

"Sleep in heavenly peace..."

Alan went down to the floor with one blow. A tray of pudding clattered to the floor. Lisa shrieked and knelt beside Alan. Stella started giggling. And the room filled with Rhodes and Stones and shouting.

"Someone get a towel, if he bleeds on Mom's floor she's gonna be pissed."

"Alan, are you okay?"

"This is the best Christmas ever."

"We wish you a Merry Christmas..."

From behind him, Sherriff Jason Stone said lowly, "Sorry, man, but I'm gonna have to take you downtown," as the handcuffs clicked on his left wrist.

"And a Happy New Year..."

But it was Lisa on the floor holding a towel tenderly to Alan the Weasel's face that seared him. The disappointment in her eyes when she looked up that gutted him as he put his other hand behind his back.

"We won't go until we get some..."

He shouldn't have come back. He didn't know how to do this. How to be part of a normal

Christmas. A family.

Jail, he could do.

An hour later, Joe stared blankly at the concrete wall in front of him. His life was officially a disaster. He had figgy pudding on his shoe, his fake beard itched, and "Jingle Bells," the last song he heard as he was stuffed into the front seat of the sheriff's off duty vehicle, was stuck in his head. The car, a cherry red '66 Shelby, was a beauty and in other circumstances, would have been a sweet ride. Stone had taken the cuffs off him so Joe could wave to any kids they passed on the way to town. Whether Joe wanted to wave or not. The sheriff hadn't wanted to be known as the cop who arrested Santa Claus on Christmas Eve. Joe was disinclined to argue with him.

He scrubbed his hands over his beard, unable to work up the energy to take off the damn suit. Nobody had read him his rights or given him a phone call. He supposed that was how they did things in small towns. It wasn't like he'd ever been arrested before, so what did he know? He had no one to call anyway.

It seemed pretty stupid now, thinking he could just show up and ho-ho-ho his way back into Lisa's good graces. He's lucky nobody had punched him back.

"Well, Santa, you certainly know how to liven up a party."

Lisa's voice, unexpected as it may be, brought his focus to the bars.

He stood. "What are you doing here?"

She was bundled up in a long black coat, hat, and scarf. Next to her, Stone held her elbow in one hand, an old-fashioned key ring in the other. Snow crystals clung to her hat. He'd love to have been on the outside to see her in the snow. She probably caught snowflakes on her tongue.

Jason unlocked the cell and slid the door open, then closed her inside with Joe. "Santa, I trust you'll stay on the Nice List for the rest of the night." To Lisa, "I'll be at my desk. Rattle the cage when you want out."

"Thanks." When he was gone, she turned her attention to Joe. "So...what's a nice guy like you doing in a place like this?"

"Are you okay?" he asked. The worst part about being arrested had nothing to do with being in jail. No, the worst part was imagining what the weasel had said to her before he'd gotten there. Before he shut him up.

She unwrapped her scarf. "I'm fine. Alan's fine too, in case you're wondering."

"I'm not. Why was he there?" Why had her family, so protective of her, allowed him so close?

She pulled off her hat and stuffed it into the pocket of her coat. Like she was staying there for a while. He didn't know what possessed Stone to let her even come in here, but jail was no place for Lisa. "He was there to apologize to me. Why were you there?"

Apologize.

Huh.

Christmas miracles and all that shit.

"So I hit him while he was making amends?" That was not his best move.

She nodded. "He was being nice. For a weasel." Her crooked smile nearly broke him. "Why were you there, Joe?

He slumped back onto the bench, forgetting his padding and almost tipping over. "It doesn't matter."

She crossed the room slowly, untying the belt of her long coat. "I think it does." She stopped in front of him and slid the coat off her shoulders, revealing a very sexy red nightie trimmed with white fur.

He couldn't swallow. He couldn't breathe. He couldn't figure out what the hell was going on.

Red. She was wearing red. And not much of it.

She'd gone out like that? She would have frozen. What if her coat had come open and exposed her again? She'd braved frostbite and a second humiliation for him?

While his mind tried to catch up, she sat on his lap. "I hope it's not too late to tell you what I want for Christmas, Santa Baby."

His mind was fuzzy, but his hands knew what to do, instantly skimming her sexy curves and holding her so she wouldn't fall. Or get away. He looked at the door. "What about –?"

"Stella's got it handled. Nobody will bother us until I rattle the cage."

"You shouldn't be here." He squeezed her tighter, unable to let her go. "Who knows who's been in here? It's not sanitary or safe."

She petted his beard and smiled. "They don't

actually use this cell anymore, Sarge. It's just for show. The real jail is down the hall."

This wasn't a real jail cell? "Am I really under arrest?"

She shrugged. "Probably not? I'm not sure. I think it depends on your behavior. You're actually not the first of us to grace this cell. Both my brothers—even my dad one 4th of July—have gotten a cool down period in here. I think Jason put Stella back here one night. I'm pretty sure it's not legal. But at least you're in good company."

He didn't understand. She should hate him. Her family should hate him. He'd left her and when he got smart enough to come back, he started a brawl at Christmas. With a guy who was trying to apologize—an apology she really needed to hear.

"Are you ready to listen to my wish list, Santa?"

He risked a glance at her sexy Mrs. Claus cleavage. Bad idea. He was ready to peel off both their costumes and take her right there. Reading his mind, she took off his hat and ran her fingers through his hair. Her eyes sparkling with mischief. It was a good look for her. He wanted to see it again. Every day.

"Yeah, what do you want for Christmas?" He'd give it to her. Whatever it was. "You want the moon?"

She shifted in his lap as she shook her head, her bottom rubbing him just the right way.

"I'll lasso it for you." He was no George Bailey, but he'd find a way to be her small-town hero.

"I don't want the moon. I want to know why you came back tonight."

"That's all?"

"No, but that's a good place to start."

Nothing about her was blending into their surroundings now. She was wearing red—his new favorite color—standing out, making herself seen. For him. He didn't deserve her trust—but apparently, he had it. He didn't deserve her love, but he was going to go after that too.

He took her hand in his. "I came back tonight, dressed like this, to steal your heart."

She laid her head on his shoulder. "I came here tonight, dressed like this, to give it to you."

She felt so right. Everything in his life suddenly felt so right. Could it really be this easy? "I'm not good enough for you, but I'm selfish enough to not care."

She lifted her head up. "Why do you say that? That you're not good enough?"

"I just got arrested in your mother's kitchen."

"I don't think you're really under arrest."

There was a special place in hell for having hard-on in a Santa suit. He was sure of it. "I'm too old for you."

"I think you'll do just fine keeping up with me, gramps."

He was so ready to whisk her away, but he needed to know she wasn't going to come around to all their challenges and leave him when she figured it out. It would hurt now. It would kill him later.

He didn't want to tie her down now. Make her think her world was confined. Getting that apology from the weasel might have freed her up to try more wild and crazy things. "Seriously, mistletoe. You're young. You've still got some exploring to do. Some more things to try that are unexpected."

"So do them with me."

He thought of her parents—her whole family. How they took care of each other, worked as a unit. She'd expect that from him. "I don't know how to love."

"Yes you do. You so do. Do you think I could be here now, dressed like this, putting myself out there to be seen if I didn't think my heart was safe?" She placed his hand on her chest. "You give love just fine. You just don't know how to accept love. But I can give you that."

He swallowed past a lump in his throat that threatened the first tears in three decades. She could give him that. He just had to let her.

"I don't have a job—"

She interrupted him. "You can sell pot-holders!" She tugged on his beard. "I knew you'd come back, you know."

"Oh really? I didn't know—how did you figure it out?" How could she trust him so much when he didn't trust himself?

"I just knew. I even told Stella this morning."

He kneaded her thigh. Because he could. Because he was beginning to understand that this wasn't a dream. She was here, flesh and blood and in his arms. And she wanted him. She wanted to give him her heart. "So what was all that business about wanting me to be a temporary lover? That you wouldn't have slept with me if I were staying?" He dipped down and inhaled the scent of her neck. "You had me fooled."

"I changed my mind."

"You changed your mind?" Like it was just that easy.

"I want you to stay. I want to see where this goes. I just want you for Christmas. Maybe every Christmas."

Every Christmas. Every Christmas sounded just fine to him. He cupped her cheek in his hand. "I can give you that."

And then he brought out the sprig of mistletoe he'd put in his pocket so many hours ago, held it above their heads, and kissed his naughty *and* nice Mrs. Claus to fill in the rest of the words he wasn't sure he knew how to say.

Yet. He figured he had plenty of time. He had every Christmas after all.

Sneak Peek

If you enjoyed *When It's Love*, you don't want to miss the next Silver Pines story.

All I NEED

Stella Franklin isn't the same awkward, nerdy girl she'd been in high school, but try telling that to her family. Her sister won't stop bugging her about bringing a date to her upcoming posh wedding, so Stella makes up a teensy weensy white-lie to get Bridezilla off her back—a boyfriend named Garrett Tanaka D.V.M—a man she saw on a website.

Too bad (before she "breaks up" with him) her imaginary beau shows up in Silver Pines, in the flesh and smoking hot beneath his smoldering horn-rimmed glasses and honest-to-God pocket protector.

Now he's her temporary boss, her fake boyfriend (though he doesn't know it), and the very real object of her forbidden fantasies. Something about the way her very own Clark Kent comes off so mild-mannered and unassuming makes her want to rip off his glasses, rile him up, and make him lose control.

But her reluctant suitor might not be as unassuming as she thinks—and when he catches her in her lies, revenge of the nerd has never been so sexy.

Please enjoy the excerpt from *All I Need*, coming in winter of 2017...

THERE IS A big difference between bukkake and baklava.

One is appropriate for dessert at my sister's wedding shower and the other is a word I'm not even sure why I know. (That's a lie. The answer is porn.) But I offered the wrong one as a suggestion to my sister on the phone and now Megan is listing all the reasons that I won't be in charge of her shower despite the fact that I am the only person in her bridal party who actually knows how to have fun.

Not that my bukkake is my idea of fun. But I really thought she'd like the baklava suggestion since her fiancé is Greek. It was an honest mistake. Slip of the tongue.

Freudian slip of the tongue, perhaps.

We've moved on and I'm only half listening to her as she yammers on about her upcoming wedding, which is still a month away, but which my entire family has been at DEFCON status for the entire engagement. She'd been sweet and biddable, made soft by love, for about four hours after the proposal under the Christmas tree. Since then—crazy woman walking.

"But I *need* to know who you're bringing, Stella. I have to know if he is going to sit at the bridal party table with us, or if he will be sitting at a guest table."

What she means is: Will he be good enough to sit at the bridal table?

And the answer is most likely not.

I love my sister. I just love her more when she's not engaged to be married. Megan has always been high maintenance, but the very second her fiancé Brad slid that ring on her finger, she turned into a raging 'zilla. I am so, so tired of talking about this wedding. About dresses. Cakes. Flowers. Chair covers. Bows. Tulle. All of it.

Except maybe bukkake. I could probably talk about that for a little while longer without being bored.

One more month. If I don't kill my sister before June is up, it will be a miracle. I go back to half listening and pull up another veterinary clinic's website to research.

"Also, your breasts are a disaster."

Well, that gets my attention. "Excuse me? What's wrong with my breasts?" I look down. I think they are rather impressive, actually. Megan is probably just jealous because she is built more like our mom, which works out pretty well for her most of the time. Being a size six, Megan has a classic beauty and lean figure. I, on the other hand have been built like a brick house since the age of twelve. And it wasn't until I turned twenty that I learned how to use my curves to my advantage. (I also have no idea what brick houses have to do with women's figures so I'm going to add that to my Things to Google list.)

"The dress shop is having a really hard time getting your dress to fit correctly," Megan says.

"Well, you should've thought of that before you asked me to be one of your bridesmaids." *Or before you picked the plunging neckline dresses.*

I will admit that I'm sort of the family fuck up, but I will not have my lovely lady lumps blamed for it.

She goes back to centerpieces, so I go back to web browsing. Dr. Bright, my boss, wants to revamp our own veterinary clinic site, so I'm researching clinics in Seattle, the closest metropolitan area to our small Northwest town of Silver Pines, WA.

I have a pretty good idea of how I want the site to look, but it never hurts to check out the comparable ones.

"Also, he needs to wear a suit and tie. Not Dockers and a T-shirt."

"Who does?"

"Oh my God, Stella. Your date. Your date for my wedding."

Oh yeah, him.

I don't actually have a date for my sister's wedding, yet. I don't have any real prospects, either. I've been…busy. Between work and my side business, I don't have much time for wedding date hunting. And, well, eligible bachelors are officially on the endangered species list in small town Silver Pines.

We are only eighteen miles from a college town, so there are plenty of cute guys, but they are all twenty-two and under. And I am too busy to add babysitting a boyfriend to my to-do list.

And most of the time, I am fine with that. Really.

"Hey, Megan. I really need to get back to work. Can we talk about this later? I'll call you tonight and you can tell me all the things that are wrong with my boobs then, okay?"

Because the conversation is going to happen whether I want it to or not, but I can at least show up armed. Wine and fuzzy slippers, are the preferred armor when it comes to Megan, but even just being home would be an improvement.

I let my attention drift back to my monitor. According to the website, Dr. Rivers, one of Doc B's friends, took on a new vet. I wish Doc B would be like her friend and get some help. Another vet would sure take some of the pressure off her. As it is, I pretty much handle her personal life scheduling or she'd neglect to have one. Leann Bright is a fabulous animal doctor, but she totally sucks at things like eating regular meals and getting her hair cut. I have resorted to filling her Netflix queue and forcing her to take time for relaxing.

This guy...Garrett Tanaka, DVM...is an interesting character. The picture is grainy, so maybe he isn't as dorky as he appears. But, wow, look at those glasses. Thick, black...Clark Kent would be jealous.

"What about Cole? I bet he'd be your date." Megan asks, not ending the call as I'd hoped.

Ugh. Cole? Not a chance.

"Have you suffered a blow to your head recently, Megan? Cole and I broke up." For many, many good reasons.

"Well, he's still friends with Brad. I'm sure you guys could get along for one day. Besides, maybe you could patch things up. Wouldn't that be romantic? Getting back together at my wedding. I mean, weddings bring out—"

"No!" I don't mean to yell, but hell-to-the-no.

Cole is not in my get-your-life-together-Stella plan. I am five months into the Year of Stella and the return of Cole would be a serious step backwards.

"Cole was horrible for me."

"Well, there is something to be said for bad boys."

"Bad boys, yes. Mean boys, no. Besides, what do you know about bad boys? Brad is like Saltine cracker boring."

"I don't even know what that means, but Brad is not boring. And I just don't want you to end up alone."

What Megan doesn't want is for me to embarrass her. But she'll never get her wish because no matter how I try not to be, I have always been an embarrassment to Megan. I tend to "draw attention" which is code speak for "spectacle."

For most of my life, I wanted to be like Megan. Hell, I wanted to *be* Meg. Megan is classy. Poised. Stylish. Thin. She manages to live her life without a hair out of place, a broken nail, or a bead of sweat.

I am the opposite of her in every way. It isn't just my curves, though my size has always been part of the gulf between us. No, it's more. I can't contain myself the way Meg does, to my sister's utter chagrin. And the harder I try to be "normal" the more I stick out and embarrass us both.

"What you need to do is find a boyfriend. You know if you just—"

"Don't start, Meg." I'm so tired of conversations that start with "if you just."

"I want you to be happy. Snagging a man isn't brain surgery, you know. You're a great girl. If you just—"

Desperate to cut her off, I blurt out, "I'm seeing somebody!"

Why did I say that?

God, now what? Damage control is key here. Because Megan is a cunning opponent in the game of wits.

"It's new. I haven't told anyone yet because we're …trying to…um…take it slow. You know, nurture it a little."

I want to hit my head on the desk. *Why can't you control your mouth?* Stupid. Stupid and nothing good this way comes. I know Megan won't let it go.

"Who is he?"

I cover the mic on my phone. "What? What? Megan, you're breaking up. Are you going through a tunnel?"

"Nice try."

Think Stella. "I told you that we're keeping this on the down low for now. He's just out of a bad relationship, too." That seems plausible, right? For this guy who I'm completely making up to be nursing a broken heart?

"At least tell me his name."

I look around the reception area for a lifeline, my eyes settling on my monitor and Dr. Rivers' website. "Garrett. His name is Garrett."

"Oh, I like that name. Where did you meet him?"

"The internet?" That isn't a lie exactly.

"The internet? Seriously, Stella?"

God it's like my sister is stuck in the '90s. "Yes, the internet. It's this thing where you can communicate with people all over the world through a little box in your house or sometimes your phone."

"Funny. What's he like? Where is he from?"

I look at the fuzzy picture, tilting my head sideways and then back. I can't tell her that he's grainy or black and white. "He's kind of serious." Nobody else would look that earnest in thick glasses. "But he's great with animals." Probably. "He lives in Seattle."

"Well, he must be a vet then, if you know he's good with animals."

"Or maybe, Nancy Drew, he's just an animal lover." I check the time; lunch is almost over. "I really have to go. Appointments start soon."

"Okay...but call me later."

"Right." Right after I get that lobotomy I need.

I'm attempting to open a cantankerous bottle of wine when I hear the knocking on my apartment door. I'm not expecting anyone, but am thrilled to see my best friend's face through the peephole.

I open the door wide and thrust the bottle I'm holding, corkscrew and all, into Prita's hands. "Thank God you are here. I thought I was going to have to resort to drinking cooking sherry."

Prita rolls her eyes and takes the bottle into the kitchen. "Just so you know, I'll open this, but I am mad at you." She pierces me with a look edged with grit. "What the hell, Stella? I thought I was your best friend?"

"Don't stop with the bottle, but tell me what you are talking about." I get down two glasses and ignore her attempt to intimidate me. I'm well used to her grit and it doesn't bother me. "I've had a really long day."

She shoots me another look like she's forgotten that I'm not afraid of her. So I shrug. She looks at the bottle in her hand and screws up her face. "What did you do to this poor cork?" she asks, honestly perplexed at its state of uncorkiness despite still being fully lodged inside the neck of the bottle. "I thought we bought you the screw top wine?" S*o this wouldn't happen* she leaves off because I'm not nearly as good at opening wine as I am consuming it.

I take the now opened bottle, bless her heart, and begin pouring. "We did. But I ran out and I had this bottle in the cupboard or cooking sherry left."

"You literally live above a bar."

"I know, but Max looks at me funny when I wear my bunny slippers downstairs, and I was in no mood to put real people clothes back on." I take a healthy, unclassy swig. "Now, why are you mad at me again?"

Prita grabs her own glass and settles onto my couch, pushing away all the sequined pillows until they tumble to the floor.

I join her, setting the bottle on the end table next to her and plopping my bunny slippered feet onto the coffee table. "You have side bangs today," I notice aloud.

"Don't distract me. I'm mad at you."

"So you keep saying." I would kill for Prita's hair.

Though, to be honest, Prita is willing to spend a whole lot more money on hair product than I am. But hers is so soft and never flat. Just long waves of rich brown that are never out of place and never frizzy. Unlike my hair which is also brown but never in place and always frizzy.

She lets out a beleaguered sigh meant to guilt me into submission. It would probably work on other people. Just not me. "Imagine my surprise when I opened Facebook to see Megan posting something that was *not* about her wedding."

"That is weird." I muted my sister's Facebook posts in an effort to not strangle her with a wedding veil, so I haven't seen what Megan's been putting down for three months or so.

"Right? Her update was instead about how happy she is about her baby sister and her new *beau*. What the hell, Stella? And who calls men *beaus?*"

Unease, an old friend of mine, settles itself into my shoulders, tightening all the muscles around my neck into bands of stress. What part of "keeping it on the down low" does Megan not understand? She's posting about my fake boyfriend now?

I quickly open the app on my phone to see what kind of damage she's wrought.

Prita huffs at being ignored. "Explanation please. I thought we discussed way back in middle school that BFF trumps sister when it comes to boy news. There was a pinky swear involved and now you hurt my feelings. Why don't I know about this new boy? I thought you were not dating because this was the Year of Stella or some damned thing."

"It is and I'm not." I read the post. Megan didn't post particulars. She referred to Garrett as "G" and was coy about answering everyone else's query. Which of course, is making them more ravenous for details. Which of course was Megan's goal. Which of course means I am screwed.

I meet Prita's scrutinizing gaze. "I don't even know what to say. I don't suppose we can just drop this and pretend it didn't happen."

Prita isn't so mad that she doesn't refill my glass. "No I don't suppose we can."

I put my phone down and gulp more wine. As far as humiliations go, this one just might rival my spring break shenanigans caught on camera on *Wild and Crazy Girls: Ft. Lauderdale*. Lifting my shirt and showing my ta-tas for a trucker hat hadn't been my idea, but I'd gone along with it willingly. What were the odds that that particular DVD would end up being shown at a bachelor party attended by every man in Silver Pines, including my dad and brother?

"I'm waiting..."

I sigh. Back to the present day humiliation. "She was being unreasonable."

"Megan?"

I nod. "She wanted me to ask Cole to be my date for the wedding."

"Gross."

"Right? So, I just wanted to throw her off track to buy some time. I don't even know how or why I said it, actually, but I told her I met someone."

"But you haven't."

I shoot Prita a "seriously?" look. "I'm not even

going to dignify that." I tap my nails on the glass. "Let's just ignore the Facebook thing. It will go away on its own. I'll break up with Garrett before the wedding and everything will be fine."

Prita executes a perfect hair flip. I do not know why. It's not like there are any men in the room to hypnotize with the power of her hair. "You named your fake boyfriend Garrett?"

"I was looking at some guy's picture at the time. He's a new vet in Seattle. His name is Garrett."

Prita settles into the cushions and fixes me with a calm I'm-your-therapist stare. Except she's not anybody's therapist because she decided to hell with her college degree and bought a coffee shop instead. "What does he drive?"

"My fictitious suitor? What do you want him to drive?"

Prita purses her lips in thought. "I think he drives a Ferrari."

I laugh. "The man in the picture is definitely more of a sedan guy. Probably beige. With really good mileage."

"How did you meet him?"

"Oh, the internet."

"Nice. Maybe I should make up a boyfriend, too. Get Mummie off my back."

"Good plan. Maybe they can be friends. Garrett and Roger."

"I don't want to date anyone named Roger."

Oh, I know. Because Prita wants to date my brother Jason. She just won't admit it.

We finish the wine and I send Prita downstairs to

grab a ride from Max, my landlord and the owner of the pub I live above. Max will get her settled because that is what Max likes to do.

As I get ready for bed, I add "break up with imaginary boyfriend" to my to-do list for sometime in the next couple of days and everything will be fine. Nobody pays that much attention to Megan anyway.

Wait, Don't Go

Never miss a release, freebie, or sneak peek at what's happening in the world of Gwen Hayes. Subscribe today and get a free eBook.
gwenhayes.com/news
Or visit me at gwenhayes.com

About the Author

Gwen Hayes lives in the Pacific Northwest with her real life hero, their children, and the pets that own them. She writes stories for teen and adult readers about love, angst, and saving the world.

Gwen's first novel, *Falling Under*, was released in March of 2011 by NAL/Penguin and followed up by the sequel, *Dreaming Awake*, in January of 2012.

In addition to writing, Gwen is a freelance editor at www.fresheyescritique.com.

She is represented by Jessica Sinsheimer of the Sarah Jane Freymann Literary Agency.

Made in the USA
San Bernardino, CA
15 November 2016